APR   2016

D0830241

DAVID FOSTER WALLACE RUINED
MY SUICIDE

AND OTHER STORIES

D. D. Miller

DAVID FOSTER WALLACE RUINED

MY SUICIDE

AND OTHER STORIES

A Buckrider Book

© D.D. Miller, 2014

No part of this publication may be reproduced, stored in a retrieval system or transmitted, in any form or by any means, without the prior written consent of the publisher or a license from the Canadian Copyright Licensing Agency (Access Copyright). For an Access Copyright license, visit www.accesscopyright.ca or call toll free to 1-800-893-5777.

Buckrider Books is an imprint of Wolsak and Wynn Publishers.

Cover image: Jodie Griggs, GettyImages
Cover and interior design: Marijke Friesen
Author photograph: Neil Gunner
Typeset in Sabon
Printed by Coach House Printing Company Toronto, Canada

The publisher gratefully acknowledges the support of the Canada Council for the Arts, the Ontario Arts Council and the Canada Book Fund.

Buckrider Books
280 James Street North
Hamilton, ON
Canada L8R 2L3

Library and Archives Canada Cataloguing in Publication

Miller, D.D., 1976–, author
David Foster Wallace ruined my suicide and other stories / D.D. Miller.

ISBN 978-1-894987-84-4 (pbk.)

I. Title.

PS8626.I445D39 2014   C813'.6   C2014-900351-X

To three amazing women:
Barbara Sheffield, Judy Miller and Jan Dawson

CONTENTS

DAVID FOSTER WALLACE
RUINED MY SUICIDE

1. August 2008

I had a problem with endings. I couldn't finish anything. And I'm convinced that it all started with my name: Gregor Postma. I go by Greg, which is even less complete, but the only people who ever called me Gregor were my Dutch father and grandmother. My grandmother died long ago and, at that point, I hadn't seen my father in a decade, so sometimes, when I saw "Gregor" printed on a bill or when a telemarketer called and asked for me by that name, I was surprised by how incomplete it sounded.

Subways, I'd discovered, offered false endings. They get to an end only to turn around and continue. Riding the subway was as close to a hobby as I had back then. I liked that feeling of always going somewhere. I'd ride in the front car sometimes all the way to the final station, then get out and walk to the other end of the train so I would still be in the front. I'd sit in the very front seat by the grimy window with the driver hidden away in the cockpit to my right, looking for the end of the line. It's awkward to stare out the front window of the subway because the seats face the wrong way, and the movements of the train are much more deliberate in that car – the shifts in speed, the bumps and jumps are all exaggerated – but I'd been riding that way for a long time, almost daily since I'd been relieved of my duties from my job with the Chindigo bookstore chain.

Rumours were that there were plenty of jumpers in Toronto. With all my riding of the subway, I thought I would have seen at least a few. But I hadn't yet. The closest I'd come was seeing a man try to jump.

I saw him as soon as the light of the station appeared during the train's approach through the tunnel. He was standing very close to the end of the platform, too close to the edge, leaning out over the track and staring into the tunnel. Seeing the approaching train, he turned and walked toward the wall and then quickly paced back to the edge of the platform as the light of the station poured into the train. My heart raced. I couldn't swallow. I gripped the back of the seat as we approached the end of the tunnel, and I wondered if the jumper would hit the front of the car, exploding the glass of the window, or if he'd just fall to the tracks and be torn apart by the moving train.

And then, at the last possible moment, he turned around, and the train passed him by before coming to a rumbling stop.

I closed my eyes for the duration of the station stop. Had to take deep breaths to calm myself, to slow my beating heart.

I don't know what led me to look at that particular shelf, but one morning, I noticed a gaping hole in my book collection: a David Foster Wallace book. Immediately, I remembered lending it to Brie, a girl I'd been kind of dating a year before. As with many things that disappeared from my apartment during that time, the book ended up in her blue MEC backpack. Her backpack had a cartoonish capacity, and she took it with her always, to the numerous lessons her stereotypically overbearing Asian immigrant parents made her attend or just to meet up with friends. It was her "home away from the home I hate," she always said.

The last time I saw Brie was at the lake in Sunnyside Park by the western beaches. She was skating with a pack of roller derby girls, wearing what looked to be brand new roller skates.

I was sitting in the grass near the path when she skated by, and she didn't notice me. She was holding the hands of another skater and looking straight into her eyes as they skated. I didn't recognize the look completely, but sort of. I'd almost seen it before, only a few months previous. She'd almost looked at me like that. But not quite.

In early spring of 2008, a new bookstore, Zed's, opened up a few subway stops away from my apartment. It seemed strange. New bookstores just weren't appearing, and even franchises like Chindigo didn't seem too concerned with selling books anymore. Trash still sold: ultra-violent detective books, pseudo-porn for middle-aged women, cartoonishly gory sci-fi or fantasy series for young adults. But more and more sales were of perfumy soap, French presses, throw rugs, kids' toys.

Next to Zed's there was a building that had been badly damaged by fire and was boarded up. On the plywood where the front door would have been, someone had hastily spray-painted "dont die" in drippy black lettering.

The bookstore was tiny, just a single room with bins full of paperbacks in the middle. The walls were lined floor to ceiling with shelves of neatly packed hardcovers and trade paperbacks. There were very few sections: fiction, non-fiction and comics/graphic novels. No subdivisions within. The owner was a fifty-something man with thin-ning, saltnpeppery hair. He was so thin he was almost gaunt and always dressed in fading, tight black denim and T-shirts that were mostly plain and dark. He smiled upon arrival and departure, but in all the visits I'd made to the store, I'd never spoken to him and had never found any-thing to buy. Not because there wasn't anything I didn't like, but because I rarely found anything I didn't already own.

I entered the store and walked slowly along the fiction wall, lazily scanning the names until I got to *W*. There were four Wallace works on the shelf: *The Broom of the System*, *Infinite Jest*, *Brief Interviews with Hideous Men* and *Oblivion: Stories*. The same four sitting on the shelf in my apartment.

I approached the desk. The man's eyes trailed as he finished reading a line.

"I'm wondering if you have any other David Foster Wallace books tucked away other than what's on the shelf?" I shrugged back toward fiction.

"It should be there, in fiction. We should have them all."

I glanced over my shoulder back toward the section. "I was just over there."

"I'm pretty sure," he said. "I'd be surprised. Which one?"

"*Girl with Curious Hair*," I said.

His eyebrows dipped inward; he shifted off his stool and closed his book. It was an old paperback version of John Barth's *The Floating Opera*. I'd never read it.

The man hurried over to the fiction wall and stood in front of the Ws as I had only a few moments before. He returned.

"You're right," he said, settling back on his stool behind the counter. "I could have sworn we had a copy of it. Sworn. I'm really sorry." He shook his head and slouched sadly.

"It's okay," I said. "Honestly. It must be hard to keep his books in. Perhaps you sold it," I said, feeling as if I were comforting him. He just shook his head, staring down at the counter.

I told him "thank you" and exited, heading back across the street and into the subway. When I got there, I walked all the way down the platform to where I knew the front of the train would stop.

Mi-young was eighteen years old, lived in Mississauga and was saving money to go to university. That was all I'd ever learned about her life.

I sat down at my computer desk and typed in the URL: http://www.camtogether.com/private-group/mi-young

The screen faded up on Mi-young. She sat in a big comfy chair. The camera didn't show much else behind her: the top of a bookshelf up against a white wall, the books just far enough away that the titles were illegible. She was sitting with her long legs wrapped under her in the comfortable, contortioned pose of the young. She was in pale blue running shorts and a white tank top.

I had to share Mi-young with others. Anyone who kept their CamTogether account up to date could join in with any of the girls. I tried to ignore them, pretend that they weren't there, but she often said our usernames when one of us typed something she found amusing. She had regulars, like me, but I tried not to remember their names.

Mi-young was Korean-Canadian. She was tall, thin, but athletic. Her skin was a lovely shade of olive. Her breasts were small but seemed to be the perfect size for her frame and her nipples were long and surprisingly pale.

She'd already started touching herself by the time I'd logged in. The arm of her tank top was tugged aside to expose her left breast. Her fingers slid down her inner thigh and flicked along the edges of her underwear. She spread her knees and she blew me a kiss, winking slowly. I could swear she was looking right at me. I felt as if I could see my reflection in her open eye.

I eventually broke down and bought a new copy of the Wallace book. The independent bookstore in the Annex didn't have *Girl with Curious Hair*, so I was forced to go to Chindigo. The location I had worked at was a large, multi-storey location in a fairly upscale mall on Bloor Street at Bay. I shuddered when I entered, literally, and got the tinge of a headache from the overwhelming scent of the soaps and candles that had begun to take up more and more of the store's retail space.

I recognized a few of the staff members, but there was a constant rotation of "booksellers" and they all had a tendency to look the same: thick-rimmed glasses, slim corduroys, some kind of ironic and/or band T-shirt under the company-issue blue vest. One person I knew I would recognize was my nemesis, Karen Sears, the floor manager, and a dedicated Chindigo lifer. She'd always hated me, hated my obsession with David Foster Wallace and the whole postmodern experiment. She was the person who fired me, and she seemed to take great pleasure in telling me that I didn't have "the Chindigo attitude." I didn't interact well with customers, she told me. I was rude. Sarcastic.

I quickly made my way to the fiction section. The edition of *Girl with Curious Hair* on the shelf was a reprint edition; an ugly, piss-yellow version with what looked like an image of splattered molasses on it. The copy I'd lost was the 1989 trade version with the black and white image of a woman on it with her head thrown back. I grabbed the book and headed for the cash registers.

Only metres away, I spotted Karen Sears coming up the stairs directly in front of me. I quickly slid to the ground in the Home Repair section. It reminded me of the times Brie would come to visit, and we'd make a game of trying to kill my entire shift without being seen by Karen. We'd hide out in obscure corners of the store (like the poetry corner), and Brie would ask me endless questions about university, though none of her questions seemed particularly important: What did English professors wear? Did we just sit around tables and argue about stuff? Were there bells like in high school to tell you when your class ended?

I turned my head and noticed I was next to a small section of books on knots. I grabbed one called *Book of the Knot*. I sprung the book open at about the middle to a section on nooses. While the hangman's knot was central, there was an array of styles displayed that I hadn't been aware of: the slip knot, the tarbuck, the bowline. I studied the images, enthralled by the slight variations, the extra loops, the tricks. I sat transfixed at the tangled beauty of them. I'm not sure how long I sat there, but when I remembered to stand up and look for Karen, she was nowhere to be seen.

I replaced the *Book of the Knot* and scurried to the cash registers.

The beginning of the end of Brie and me came on a blazing hot day early in the August of the summer we spent together. Brie and I decided to meet up in the Annex, close to her place. I'd just met up with her, and she was on her roller skates gliding comfortably next to me on the Bloor Street sidewalk. Brie wore a pair of her mother's old blue roller skates that she'd found buried deep in a closet. They were worn and tattered and had chipped wheels, but she never went anywhere without them and was comfortable enough on them to scoot around people, transition quickly and expertly, and then skate backwards in front of me at times.

We could hear them coming before we saw them. Ahead of us, the crowds parted on the wide sidewalks. There was the sound of many wheels grinding on pavement, and a din of voices as well. Suddenly the sidewalk ahead of us was emptied of walkers, and they were directly in front of us: a pack of five women on roller skates, but as different from Brie's old-school quads as they could get; theirs were slick-looking and modernized, black leather low-cut boots on gleaming metal trucks. The girls were upon us quickly, shoving fliers into our hands before isolating and circling Brie.

"Holy shit! Those are so cool!" said a skater in jean shorts and a tight tank top with a skull logo on the chest. She even bent down to touch Brie's old skates. "I can't believe you can still skate in those things."

"You're a total derby girl," another said definitively. They were a mix of women: black, white, tall, short, skinny, shapely. They all looked very confident on their skates and they seemed very disinterested in me. Brie looked shocked.

Finally one of the girls stepped forward and pointed at the fliers they'd given us. "You need to come check out a bout." The flier was an advertisement for a game in the Toronto Roller Derby League. "Maybe you could even get some new skates," she said before skating away with the others and leaving us alone on the sidewalk.

After a few seconds of odd silence, people began to filter around us again. Brie just stood there, so tall on her skates, staring down at the flier and the women pictured on it: two women in full gear, hair flailing from under stickered helmets, fishnets and tights torn and ragged, skating into each other shoulder to shoulder, looks of violent determination etched onto their faces. She held the flier in both hands and just stared.

2. September 2008

I just happened to be walking by Zed's and decided to head in on the off chance that he had actually acquired something I didn't already own.

"Excuse me," the owner said as I entered. "Were you in a few weeks' back looking for the David Foster Wallace collection?"

I was surprised that he remembered.

"Well, wouldn't you know that a few days later someone traded in a copy." He turned quickly and headed toward the Ws and pulled the copy out from the shelf. It was the same ugly yellow edition I'd recently bought at Chindigo. "Here it is," he said proudly.

"I'm so sorry," I explained. "I found a copy elsewhere."

He stared down at the book, his smile waning. "Well, that's fine. Then I would be without a copy again, wouldn't I?"

I thanked him and exited the store, finally accepting that I would never, ever find anything at Zed's that I didn't already own.

As I passed the burned-out building on the way back to the subway, I noticed that someone had spray-painted over the original "dont die" with red spray paint. In even larger, drippier letters it now read "dont PANIC!!!"

I rode in my usual spot in the front car on the subway home. As we approached the station, and I saw people lingering near the edge of the platform, I couldn't help but hope that this time, one of them might actually jump.

Brie was much younger than I was and had just graduated from high school when I met her. She was with a bunch of other high-schoolers one night in High Park near the massive wooden children's playground at the south end of the park. I'd stumbled upon them, about ten or so young adults illuminated by cigarette butts and the odd flashlight. I just happened to have a pocketful of weed, which was all I needed to grab their interest.

Brie stood out from the freaks and geeks who made up the group. She was the only Asian; she was tall, muscular and had deep brown eyes that peeked into mine with their glittery interest, impossible to look away from. She was also extremely bright, but a little flaky and talkative because of that. She had her backpack with her that night, of course, and that pair of her mother's old roller skates slung over her shoulder. Her backpack was overflowing with clothes, books, and various other practical and impractical items, like a flute – I would later learn – and a tiny cooler that held snacks, which usually consisted of some kind of cheese. Even in that summer after her senior year of high school, she was expected to attend music lessons twice a week, on top of soccer practice and summer tutoring.

"I don't get along with my parents so much," she said when I asked her about it. We were sitting a little ways away from the main group, sharing a joint. She sucked the joint hard and then let the thick, uninhaled smoke ooze out from between her lips and slip up over her face like a veil. "They are, like, *super* strict." She handed it back to me and coughed. The smoke burst out of her mouth. I learned that the roller skates were so that she could move around the city quickly: get to her various lessons and sports practices, but also get home by her curfew. She told me that her parents had forced her into figure skating at a young age.

It was such a different story from my own that I was taken in by it. I hadn't seen my father in years at that point and, while my mother still physically existed, the woman I knew as a child – as fragile and distant as she'd seemed even then – was completely gone now.

So much about Brie seemed young. She was enthralled by the fact that I'd (until very recently) been in grad school at U of T. I didn't tell her how much I'd hated it, how much the accumulated loans were ruining my life. She'd received a scholarship to attend there the following fall. "But I don't think I want to go," she said. We'd been sitting away from her friends for quite a while and a few had begun to disperse.

"Why not?" I asked.

"I don't know what I want to do." She rolled her eyes.

"Okay, I've got some ideas about what I want to do, but there is no way my parents will let me. It's so typical, right? I've got to be a doctor or something. As long as it's got something to do with science." She sat back, her arms extended behind her and stared straight ahead. "My parents are such stereotypes that it's almost racist."

I laughed and managed to ask her what she wanted to do.

"Philosophy. Fine Arts. English. Something that will make me think about stuff."

I'd done an English undergrad because I liked to read and lacked the desire to do anything else. Pretty flimsy reasoning.

"Science will make you think," I said, remembering the wonder of Grade 10 Biology, of cutting open a frog and seeing innards that looked remarkably like miniature human innards and how that awakened in me an awareness of the interconnectedness of things.

"Oh shit!" She checked her watch and began to scramble. "Curfew." She kicked off the pair of flats she'd had on and crammed them into her backpack. "Gotta get home in like fifteen minutes."

"What's your name?" I asked. She had long, slender toes that were active in the grass: they stretched and grasped as though they were just unbound from some tight wrapping. Her toenails were unpainted and the pale whites glowed in the night.

"Brie," she said, sliding her foot into one of her roller skates.

"Bri, like Brianna?"

"No. Brie, like the cheese." With her skates secured, she pulled a small notebook and pen out of her bag. She tore out a piece of paper and scrawled her real name on it. "Find me on Facebook," she said, scampering across the grass as if she didn't have eight wheels strapped to her feet. When she finally hit the paved path, she leapt once into the air for momentum and, with smooth crossovers and long deep strides, was very quickly gone.

There'd been a delay on the subway that had left the train stranded in a dark tunnel and made me late for Mi-young's session. It almost didn't matter anymore; I could summon her image at will. There wasn't a centimetre of her body that I didn't feel I knew. An orifice that I hadn't peered into. I got home ten minutes into the session.

Mi-young was fondling herself with a tiny, buzzing machine that slid over her finger. She got an almost goofy smile on her face when she was pleasuring herself, almost like she was on the verge of laughing. Then I saw her look off-screen and smile.

"It looks like our special guest has arrived," she said.

And then the body of some guy entered the screen. His head was above the shot, cut off from view, but his body was not. He was young, also, and naked. He stood next to Mi-young.

I was baffled.

She rested her cheek against the guy's thigh and flitted her long, thin fingers over his penis. Horrified, I reached for the mouse to close the window. I tried not to, but glanced at the screen long enough to see her take him into her mouth.

Even if it was just for one summer, it's almost inexplicable that Brie and I had managed to get along for as long as we did.

I didn't have any friends and hadn't had a girlfriend since high school. We spent a lot of time together, mostly in High Park, sitting under trees smoking pot while she rambled. She was young, healthy and excited; had just finished high school and felt like she could take over the planet. While we did fool around – in the park, on the saggy couch in my musty basement apartment – it seemed forced. She was exceptionally pretty – certainly more so than any other girl I'd ever spent time with – but was young and awkward. She had a thrilling body from a lifetime of sports that she didn't seem to know what to do with. She lacked confidence about her looks, seemed clueless about her sexuality. She'd been a gangly, awkward, tomboyish kid who'd sprouted up in her late teens and had filled out into an attractive young woman.

Usually, after she went home, I'd lie in my bed masturbating and thinking about her. Thinking about the things we hadn't done.

But after meeting those roller girls, Brie went to a roller derby bout, purchased brand new roller skates, and I didn't see her much anymore. I tried texting her a few times, but she'd always text back much later, apologetic. She'd tell me that we'd get together soon, but we never did, and eventually the texts stopped. On Facebook, I saw that she'd started to train. Pictures started to pop up of her in derby gear, skating around a track in an old military hangar north of the city; then, eventually, photos of her in a team uniform and playing in games. It was hard to put these images of her next to those I had in my memory. There was a gap there somewhere.

The first thing I did on the morning I decided to kill myself was turn on the TV. There was just something about the silence in the room. I didn't check the channel. I don't even remember caring. It was just noise.

With the TV in the background I took about fifteen minutes to screw the bike hook into the ceiling. The package said it was good for ninety kilograms or two hundred pounds. Then I tied a fresh noose. I had to untie the one I'd tied the day before. I'd been practicing for a week at that point, every morning without even thinking why.

I attached the rope to the hooks, dragged over the chair from my computer desk and stood on it. It was in the kitchen, the only part of my apartment tall enough to allow for this. I poked my head through the noose. My left hand was over the top of my head. There was a moment there, when I paused.

I wasn't thinking anything. Nothing. Nothing at all. But I paused. The whole thing had taken about one hour. It was Saturday. I'd woken up at seven. I'd made coffee and taken about five minutes to drink a cup while I reminded myself of everything I'd planned to do. I pissed, and then I started. The hook, the noose. Ready. I was ready.

I don't know why I paused. But I did. And for the first time, I heard the TV. It was on one of the news channels.

"Some sad news this morning," the female anchor said. "Noted novelist, essayist and humourist David Foster Wallace was found dead last night at his home." A pause. "The forty-six-year-old writer, best known for his 1996 novel, *Infinite Jest*, reportedly hanged himself during the evening. He was found by his wife at 9:30 p.m."

I pulled my head out of the noose, stepped down from the chair. My heart wasn't necessarily racing, but it was beating very hard. It was only the second time I'd been aware of my body the whole morning. The first time was after the coffee, when I'd had to piss.

David Foster Wallace.

Dead.

Hanged himself.

From where I was standing – in the kitchen next to the chair I'd dragged from my computer desk – I could see my fiction bookshelves. There were two of them. Side by side. About six feet tall, made of that faux-oak Ikea "wood" with books stacked on top that touched the ceiling. On the bottom shelf of the second were the books by David Foster Wallace, including the ugly piss-yellow edition of *Girl With Curious Hair*.

I knew it couldn't happen like this.

"You hear that Greg Postma killed himself the other night?" I could hear the people I'd met at grad school saying. "Remember, the drop out," they'd say. And Karen Sears. I could hear her too. She'd be the one who'd make the connection if and when she ever heard the news. She'd be the first one to call me tacky. A copycat.

I looked back up at the rope hanging from the ceiling. Getting the rope down wouldn't be a problem. The hook, though, might.

I slumped down on the floor, feeling oddly hollow. Not particularly disappointed, just empty. Just something else I wouldn't be able to finish.

For days afterwards, I kept myself in motion by riding the subway for hours at a time. Sometimes from early in the morning until the sun went down.

Exiting the subway one day, I walked by Zed's Books and the burned-out building next to it. It still sat there, virtually untouched in the months since the fire. The plywood that covered the door and had been spray-painted with "dont PANIC!!!" was now covered in posters. I almost walked by without even giving the posters a thought until I noticed the roller skates.

On the poster, two stylized female cartoon characters glared at each other: one was decked out in leopard print, the other in a green, sailor-style uniform. The Toronto Roller Derby Championship was happening that weekend.

I crossed the street and entered the subway. As usual I sat in the first car at the front and stared out the window. Waiting.

The Toronto Roller Derby League played its games north of the city in the hangar in Downsview Park. It was a massive space, with huge windows that spread the late-evening summer sunshine across the hard concrete floor and the round track in the middle. Metal bleachers lined the track and they were full of a strange mix of people: punks and jocks and grandmothers and children, hipsters, nerds, a whole posse of women on a stagette. Loud rock and roll music blared from speakers sprinkled among the bleachers, and a mohawked man in a slim suit and skinny tie prowled the zone between the track and the seats, stepping over and around the people who sat on the floor lining the track. He yelled into the mic, his face beet red and eyes gleaming: I could barely make out what he said. The louder he got, the louder the crowd got.

I managed to squeeze my way onto the edge of a bleacher as team announcements were made and the two teams skated onto the track.

When the team clad in leopard print – The Gore-Gore Rollergirls – were getting their specific introduction, they huddled in a massive ball in the centre of the track and skated slowly, bobbing slightly. When one of their names was called, that skater stood and waved. I couldn't quite make out Brie in the mass of skaters, but when her name and number – Asian Sinsation 1953 – were called, she stood out wonderfully, taller on skates and more muscular than I remembered her. She stood and blew a kiss to the crowd. She really hadn't changed that much physically, but something had. Something made her almost unrecognizable.

While it seemed more organized and athletic than the '70s version of roller derby I had in my head, the game, nonetheless, looked like little more than barely controlled chaos. Brie was a phenomenal skater. Her years of figure skating making her look so comfortable on the track. She was a "blocker" from what I could gather by the announcer's ragged explanation, and her job was to hit. And she did it with a near recklessness that got her sent to the penalty box a lot yet didn't seem to affect her team: I didn't understand the scoring, but I could see on the scoreboard that her team was running away with it. The bigger the lead, the harder Brie – Asian Sinsation – seemed to hit.

At one point she took a run at an unsuspecting opponent: she caught her looking the other way and crushed her, sending her flying into the aptly named suicide seats that lined the track. The crumpled skater landed on the laps of a bunch of spectators and the crowd roared.

Brie began to skate to the penalty box when, after some discussion between her coach and one of the referees, she was thrown out of the game, the announcer explaining that she'd fouled out. On her way out she skated slowly around the edge of the track, blowing kisses to the crowd. She had a wild, gleeful expression on her face. When she skated passed me, she was so near I could have reached out and touched her. She even blew a kiss my way. But she never saw me. As she was about to exit, she stopped, turned around and made a graceful bow to the crowd.

I didn't stay for the end of the game. Downsview Park was at the northern end of the subway line. At the time, Downsview was the last subway station before the transitless sprawl beyond the city. The subway station was a major transfer point: a modern, glass-walled station ringed by bus stops. It was cavernous with the subway line deep underground. It took a long escalator ride, then another, before you got to the platform.

I was in a daze as I descended, trying to merge this new Brie with the one I'd known so briefly but – I'd thought – intensely. She'd been so naive before: a raw, unshaped human.

I'd wanted to stick around and talk to her after the game, congratulate her. But I didn't know what to say. I didn't think I'd know what to say to a woman like that, so I just slipped out while the fans counted down the final moments of the game, left with that image of her final bow and the look of pleasure on her face as she'd done it.

The subway was already pulling into the next station before I was even fully aware that I was on it. I glanced up and around me when the recorded voice came on to announce the next station. The car was almost empty. A man in steel-toed boots and paint-splattered coveralls was dozing in the far end of it; a woman in a dress suit read a paperback. I glanced forward and then back, slowly realizing that for the first time in a long time, I wasn't sitting in the front car of the train; instead, I was buried somewhere safely in the middle.

THE ILLUSION OF FLIGHT

*T*hey've spent the whole day walking through malls and packed streets. They've come all the way into town, sifted through sidewalks full of strolling tourists and rushed locals, all for a new set of Tupperware. After reading an article online about the toxicity of cheap plastic, she had concluded that all of their current plastic containers were inadequate. It's his day off, it's hot, and he wants nothing more than to sit in front of a fan with a cold beer.

The sun is glaring down at them relentlessly. People roam the streets in shorts, tank tops, almost naked, but he wears a suit because it's what she expects. He wears shoes she bought for him only two days before: black leather with pointy tips and small laces that wrap his foot tight. She wears a sundress with an elaborate floral design and thick-soled sandals. They are both thirty-four, have been married seven years and have one daughter, five, who is spending the day with her grandparents.

They finally sit down at a table outside of a café. He reaches without her seeing to adjust his shoe. He tries to loosen the laces but they are thin and hard and will not unfasten.

"I'd like an iced latte," she smiles softly. "And perhaps some carrot cake."

He forces a smile, stands, loosens his tie and wipes his forehead with his arm. He can feel a blister forming at his heel and can't move his toes.

"Jesus, it's hot."

"What was that?" She looks up at him, shielding her eyes against the glare of the sun.

Inside the café it is much cooler and the cold sucks away his sweat. Fans turn rapidly on the ceiling, and an air conditioner rattles in an open window. The interior is a vibrant mix of colours and on one wall a mural depicts dazzling yellow birds sitting in a lush green forest. The place is full of an indistinguishable mix of tourists and locals, couples and groups. Many fan themselves with pamphlets or street maps. The two teenagers behind the counter – one a blond, ponytailed girl in a short, black denim skirt with her shirt tied in a knot above her small belly – work efficiently with deadpan stares; little drops of sweat form on their faces near overworked espresso machines and small pastry ovens. The girl takes his order.

"Must be some hot in that suit," she says. When she smiles, her skin, which is bronzed from days at the beach, crinkles around her lips and chin.

He watches as she moves behind the counter. She is athletic. A soccer player, he guesses. Her legs are brown and muscled, tight raindrops for calves, funnelling down into slim, but strong, ankles. The small of her back is equally browned and a tiny valley is formed there by toned muscles. Her tan is accented by the small tattoo of a butterfly. It sits left of the centre on her back, a mix of turquoise and yellows and reds bleeding into one another on outstretched wings. As she bends and the muscles on her back contract, it gains the illusion of flight and seems beautiful to him.

When she turns back with that same sympathetic smile, he wants to tell her he thinks her tattoo is beautiful. But he feels prematurely old and restrained and embarrassed for having stared so intently so just says thank you and leaves. Outside, he is immediately overcome by the sun. The heat causes waves of distorted air to rise from the street. There is a haze embracing the downtown core that gives everything a dull, uninteresting cloak. In this part of the city – and at this time of the year – there are usually flowerpots hanging from street posts, but there have been water restrictions imposed and now the pots hold only grey and crumbling soil.

"We've got one more place to go," she says.

"Can't we just call it a day?" He sits down and slides her drink and cake across the table.

"Oh no, we'll find something." She sucks her latte through a straw.

"I'm fucking dying in this suit." He has brought his coffee to his lips, and with one sip knows he doesn't want it. It is too hot and too strong and sucks the remaining moisture from his body.

"What's that?" Her head is down as she works a white plastic fork into the cake.

He bends over with a grunt – feels the blood run to his face, his collar tighten around his neck, sweat form at his hairline – and tries once again to loosen his shoes. The laces are so thin he manages only to tighten them. "Goddamn these shoes." He wants to yell, but can only mumble under the strain.

"You're mumbling again."

He sits up and stares hard. His breath quickens. The tip of his left shoe works at the back of his right. He wants to tell her he's going home for God's sake. He's hot and tired, it's his day off, their daughter is with his parents, and he doesn't want to spend it wandering around the city looking for Tupperware.

"What's the matter, dear?"

He hates it when she uses the word "dear." It sounds unnatural and condescending. He wants to tell her she can take her Tupperware and shove it, and she can take back these shoes too, or give them to some homeless person or just throw them in the trash for all he cares. "Nothing," he finally says. "I'm just hot, that's all."

"You shouldn't've ordered coffee."

Over her shoulder he can see the girl from behind the counter. She's come outside to clean off tables. Her back is turned and he can see her tattoo.

"Next time you should order an iced latte," his wife says. "It's quite good."

He watches the wings of the butterfly move as the girl wipes a table. Her quick motions make it seem as though it's struggling to take off. One bead of sweat forms like a teardrop on its turquoise body. It runs down the girl's back and disappears under the waistband of her skirt.

SEEING YOUR OWN

He's sitting on the ground in the middle of the parking lot at the ferry terminal, leaning back against the base of a streetlight. Even from where I am standing, I can see that it's Peter Estabrooks, a guy who lived down the hall from me in residence during the first year of my undergrad degree at Simon Fraser. I am so certain it's him I have to move to get a better look.

He's decked out in the kind of clothing I see worn by the street kids downtown: faded, heavily patched pants; a huge wool sweater that is dirt stained and stretched beyond form; and a pair of combat boots that are dull, cracked and sag around his ankles. He has the same dirty blond hair and patchy beard that he had during that first winter of our undergrad lives. I remember it so vividly, my first year away from home: the quick dissolution of my parent's marriage after I'd left, the fast friendships that you think will last forever but often don't even make it through first semester.

"Dude!" he yells. "Suit-dude, spare some change man, help me get some ferry money to get to Vancouver." Peter and I didn't see each other much beyond first year. He'd gone on to an undergrad career of popularity and bar-hopping, while I'd gone on to one of trying to maintain the kind of marks that would get me into law school.

A few people shuffle around me with their heads down, ignoring this situation. I walk toward Peter, waiting for him to stop looking like a guy I'd briefly known fifteen years ago. He has these piercing blue eyes and a greyish, toothy smile that are both so familiar. When I am nearer, I see that this guy really is fifteen years younger than me and therefore can't be Peter Estabrooks. Though even up close the resemblance is striking.

"Change? Please. Can you help me out?"

My shadow swallows him as I near.

"Buddy, you all right?" he asks.

"Sorry," I mumble. I dig through my pockets and come up with a toonie, a loonie and some change. My suit suddenly feels tight. "Here," I say and hand him the money.

"Hey, thanks, man!" He fondles the coins in his calloused hands; there is dirt under his thick yellowing nails.

He looks up and smiles at me, and I turn to make my way toward the ferry. It's only as I follow the last person onto the deck of the boat that I remember that it's free to take the ferry off of the Gulf Islands. I look back in time to see the guy trudging up the parking lot toward the road, no doubt to hitch a ride somewhere. But where? I wonder. Where would a homeless man go on an island as small and quaint as this one?

I eventually lose sight of him as the ferry pulls away from the Mayne Island Terminal. Mayne Island is one of BC's Gulf Islands. I'd just spent the day with a client who – in one of his numerous eccentricities – refuses to come to Victoria. But because his wife left him for another woman awhile back, and he's now living in their tiny, uninsulated cottage in some remote corner of this remote island, we cut him some slack. Secretly I enjoy it because I love the ferry. There's just something about it. The Gulf Island ferries are small and still quaint in their overused ruggedness and salt spray–rusting kind of way. For us Vancouver Islanders, riding the ferry is the one reminder that we are actually surrounded by the ocean; you just don't get that same sense of isolation and separation when you're on a big island.

Being on a ferry and seeing this Peter Estabrooks look-alike has reminded me of a story my mother told me before she died.

After my parents divorced, my mother started to vacation at Caribbean resorts or exotic locations in Europe, which was a stark departure from the highway-motel road trips we used to take around Canada with my dad.

A little more than a year before she passed, she'd gone to Spain and had been on a ferry out to Majorca in the Mediterranean, when she saw this woman who she claimed looked just like her. It had been some loud and obnoxious Midwestern American tourist who'd talked brazenly to one of her companions the whole ferry ride. She'd apparently gone on about how her friend just *had* to go to Spain for the lovely young men and proceeded to describe how easy they were to pick up at the bars, especially in Barcelona and especially when you were an attractive middle-aged American divorcee on an extended vacation with enough cash to buy the guy a few meals and a few more drinks.

My mother told me all this in a hospital room during a particularly lucid period near the end. She told me lots of things when she was all hopped up on painkillers and feeling nostalgic for a life that was fading before her eyes.

"I regret seeing that woman," she said.

"Regret? Why?" I asked, thinking maybe she'd used the wrong word, which often happened when she was all drugged up.

"She was a version of me that could have been. She had the same hairstyle, dressed the same way, everything. It was uncanny. Like looking in a mirror. And I thought, that's how people see me. Just another middle-class divorcee prancing around Europe trying to hold on to something that's gone."

"You said she was loud and annoying," I blurted, trying to sound positive, even jokey.

But she looked away from me and out the window. "You know how they say everyone has a double in the world? Well, I don't think we're supposed to see our own. We have this image in our head that's like the perfect version of ourselves." She glanced back at me. She even reached out and took my hand. "Then when you see your double you realize it was all wrong, that image. All wrong." She looked away again. And it was terrible. Any moment of sadness, even the most abstract moment of sadness, etched into the face of someone who is dying is a horrible thing to witness. And I wish I'd told my mother she was beautiful even then (though she wasn't, really), but I didn't. I don't even remember what I said.

I look around the ferry and wonder about what she said about us all having a double. I see a woman standing alone by the railing. Her hair and the way she's dressed, even the way she is standing, reminds me of my wife. My wife is beautiful, and I don't mind saying so. She's thin in a muscular, run-five-K-a-day kind of way and has this straight, reddish-blond hair that she wears at about shoulder length and that is complemented by a sprinkle of the faintest freckles imaginable across the bridge of her nose. Also, she wears reading glasses at work and pins her hair up in a bun. She's a librarian, and, even though she won't admit it, I think she plays up the look because she likes to know that she can whip off her glasses and let down her hair when she walks away from work and turn into someone else.

The woman at the railing turns, and I see that she doesn't look like my wife: her nose is all wrong; plus, she's got too many freckles and her cheeks have too much flesh. Behind her, I see Swartz Bay and the Vancouver Island ferry terminal nearing. I stand and follow the woman to the front of the boat and line up behind her as we pull into the dock.

When I get to the office, I file the appropriate files, get a law clerk to fax off the appropriate documents, and putter around uselessly until I slip out a little early knowing full well I am incapable of getting anything else done. I just want to go home, order Korean food, sit down with my wife and watch a movie on Netflix that we've seen a million times so that halfway through we'll be so bored we'll start to fool around and have just-good-enough sex on the couch (no condom because we plan on having kids someday anyway) before we shower together and go to bed.

My wife is almost always home before me. She works for the Greater Victoria Public Library system and gets to leave at a regular hour every day. She rarely complains, seems generally content about her work and seeing her so content in her profession often makes me wonder why anyone would choose to become a lawyer. I did because my father was a lawyer and his father was a lawyer. As far as I could tell, neither was a particularly happy man: overworked, my father would come home at all hours distant and exhausted and capable of launching into a petty and useless argument with my mother at the drop of a hat. I like to think I've learned from some of my father's mistakes. I try my best not to work ten-hour days, and rarely ever work on the weekends unless it's something I can do quickly on my BlackBerry.

When I walk in the front door of our condo, my wife calls my name from the bedroom and rushes out, fumbling with an earring and dressed in a manner not befitting a lazy evening at home. Her hair is down and she is wearing a black dress that isn't too fancy, but certainly not casual. Her bare feet slap on the hardwood as she hurries toward me.

"Hey, honey." She pauses only long enough to brush her glossy, lipsticky lips across mine and keeps right on going. "Sorry, I'm running late."

"What's up?" There is something going on, and I feel like I should know, but I don't and it confuses me. The fact that she is going out hurts me way more than it should.

"I've got that Literacy Association thing, remember?" She opens up the hall closet and pulls out a pair of black shoes. "There's a Facebook event."

I remember something about an invitation now.

"I didn't realise you were going to be home so early," she says, finally getting the earring on and then bending over to put on her shoes. "You'd told me you wouldn't be able to make it."

"Right. I had a weird day and left early."

"Oh, yeah?" She comes toward me, a distracted look of faux concern on her face. "Everything okay?"

I nod. "Fine, I was just hoping to relax tonight."

"Relax away!" she says as she heads back into the bedroom. "I'll join you when I get back."

I stand dumbfounded in the hall.

"Hey! I almost forgot!" I hear her yell from the bedroom. "I saw you today." Her voice is muffled, and I can tell she is in the closet.

"Really?" I yell back.

"Yeah." She emerges from the room with a shawl around her shoulders. "Around noon, you were going into Blends on Douglas Street. I yelled but I guess you didn't hear me. By the time I crossed the street, you were gone." She stands right in front of me, and I can almost smell her shampoo though I think it might be masked by hairspray or something. "How do I look?" She spreads her arms and holds the ends of the shawl. "Will I be warm enough, you think?"

"You look great. It's nice out." I try to remember if I went into the coffee shop at all during the day. But of course, I couldn't have. "Wait, you couldn't have seen me. I was on Mayne Island until, like, three o'clock."

"Really?" She tilts her head and frowns a bit. "I was certain it was you. Same suit too." She grabs the lapel of that same suit and leans in for a kiss. "I've really got to run." She kisses me again, but I don't kiss her back.

"Of course I'm sure. I caught the nine-thirty ferry." I'm almost angry.

"Well, he looked just like you." She backs away and tugs at the shawl to straighten it. "Anyway, I won't be late. You sure you're okay?" she asks.

I shrug. "It's just been a strange day."

"Aw, I'm sorry. We'll talk about it when I get home." She kisses me yet again, on the cheek this time, and then opens the door. "Love you," she calls on the way out, and I manage to mumble the same thing back.

Since my plans are ruined, I decide to hop in the shower and wash away the day's weirdness. I run the shower hot, almost scaldingly so. Standing naked, I stare at my torso in the mirror, watching my image disappear as the bathroom steams up, and I can't help but think of the oddly coincidental conversation I've just had with my wife and how it reminds me of yet another similar event that had occurred when I was a teenager.

The last summer vacation I took with my parents turned out to be our last summer together as a family unit. I was sixteen going on seventeen and my father decided we were going to drive across the country and – much to me and my mother's horror – camp while we did it. Thankfully, my mother managed to convince my dad to stay in those generic roadside motels when the weather was bad. In many ways, I think this trip, which my mother abhorred even more than I did, may have been the final nail in the coffin for my parents' relationship. What is really sad is that, in retrospect, I think it was actually conceived as a last ditch effort to save their marriage.

About a week or so into our trip, we made it to Canada's Wonderland, the roller coaster–heavy theme park north of Toronto. We were waiting in line to go on a stand-up roller coaster when my father gasped and pointed at a kid standing by a hot dog vendor about a hundred metres away.

"Holy shit!" he said. I remember that he swore. "That kid looks just like you!"

I was already embarrassed about going on a roller coaster with my dad and now people began to shift in front of and behind us to stare. Some even glanced over at the other kid. "No, he doesn't," I said back quietly.

My father just kept looking back and forth between me and this kid. I was getting angry. The kid had the same haircut and colour, was about my height and just a little plump, not fat or anything and not exactly soft, just a little late in shedding all of his baby fat, as I'd been.

"You just think all teenagers look the same because you're old," I told my father, who was thirty-seven at the time.

He laughed. "No, really. I can't get over it. I wish your mother was here with the camera." It was terrible to think your father capable of mistaking you for someone else, and I remember wanting him to say, "Yeah, you're right," or "Except you're taller," or anything that would have shown there was some sort of father-son bond that transcended physical appearance. I remember eventually starting to think the kid did look a little like me. But I also remember thinking, quite specifically, that I was somehow better looking than he was, more stylish and cool.

My image in the mirror has completely disappeared behind the steam, and I wonder what my wife thought of that guy she saw coming out of the coffee shop earlier in the day. Was he more attractive than I was? Did he look like what she wanted me to look like?

Suddenly, I want nothing more than to see this man.

Wrapped in a towel, I head to the bedroom to get dressed. It's been hours since my wife would have seen him at the coffee shop on Douglas Street, but maybe – just maybe – if I go there and grab a coffee and walk out onto the street, I'll feel compelled to head in a specific direction, maybe even feel pulled somewhere. Or maybe he frequents that coffee shop on a regular basis and will walk in while I'm ordering.

I drop my towel and grab a fresh pair of underwear. I pull them up over my damp legs, and, suddenly, I can't help but wonder whether or not I will even be able to recognize him.

BE PREPARED

Beyond my backyard, the city ends. The sprawl comes to a sudden halt, and then there is forest. Sometimes it makes me feel like I'm on the edge of the Western world.

It's eleven in the morning. I've been up for thirty minutes, and my ears are still ringing from the band last night. I'm hungover and my hands are crammed into a sink full of a week's worth of dishes. There's a little window above my sink that looks out over my backyard. I stare out at the trees, knowing that there are already construction crews somewhere out there in the forest working to expand the subdivision.

Suddenly there is movement in the trees. A rustling of green that grows more violent until eventually my neighbour, Tom Fisher, stumbles out of the brush, flailing at cobwebs and branches. He's wearing plaid pyjama bottoms, a white undershirt and black leather sandals. And, best of all, he's carrying a gun.

Tom lives in the other half of my duplex with his wife and son. Most of my contact with him has come from the chats we've had while out in the backyard barbecuing and sipping beer, so I don't know much about him and his family. I know he's in his forties, has a beer gut like a massive ulcer and still has his hair (though it's thinning). I also know that he hasn't worked a stitch in at least a year, his wife may be the most unhappy woman I've ever met and his son is so painfully awkward that, despite being a similar age, he and my son have barely spoken.

And now I know he owns a shotgun.

As he staggers into the yard, he swats at the twigs and leaves that remain stuck to his shirt. His left slipper is half off and he's mumbling to himself. I probably have an hour or two, tops, to finish cleaning up, but I dry my hands and head to the back door.

Outside, the humidity hits me hard. It's late June and turning out to be a hot summer. I begin to sweat almost immediately, and I can smell it on my clothes, the same clothes I wore last night. The sun is to my right, and the shadow of the house is disappearing in its shift to the front.

Tom is between the light and shadow, hopping on one foot, gun tucked under his arm. His left slipper is in his hand, and he's shaking it wildly.

"Tom," I say quietly so as not to startle him. "Tom? Everything all right?"

He puts his bare foot down on the grass. His thinning hair is all askew, eyes wide open. He glances down at his foot, surprised, then drops his slipper and slides his foot back into it.

"You all right?" I ask again.

"You didn't hear?"

I shrug. "Hear what?"

"A bear," he says and motions toward the woods with the barrel of his gun.

"A bear?"

"Right! You weren't home last night. Well . . ." With his free hand he reaches into his pocket and pulls out a pack of cigarettes and lights one. "Last night, we were sitting in the living room eating dinner and we hear this scream." Tom comes right up to my back steps and rests the gun against the rail (barrel up). He leans on it, inhales deeply, squinting slightly for the smoke. "So we get up and rush to the window and I see Mrs. Dahl standing in her front yard with a lawn chair in her hand, just screaming, and her son is there on the ground – what's his name?" He stops. There are beads of sweat and little bits of dirt up on his hairline. "What's his name? The boy?"

I shake my head.

"Hmm. Feel like I should know that." He takes a drag, scratches his gut with his other hand and looks back at the woods. I can see the yellowing under the arms of his undershirt. There is a big U-shaped sweat stain on the front. I can smell the odour of beer coming off of him. Or maybe that's me. "Anyway," he continues, "I look up to where she's shaking that chair, and there's a fucking black bear running down the middle of the street! Cars are stopped, people are all coming out to see and this bear is running in circles totally confused."

"Are you serious?"

"Fuckin' right I am." He's breathing heavily and staring. "It's absolute chaos, right? Mrs. Dahl standing with a chair in her hands like it's the fucking circus; the Dahl boy – Shithead or Dingus or whatever his name is – lying on the ground, all torn up. Then the sirens." There is a wild look about his eyes that I haven't seen before. He takes a gulp of air to steady his breathing. "The bear gets right up on its back legs, right there in the middle of the street." He points toward the street out front. "Then it drops and runs between those two houses next to us and off into the woods."

"Is the boy ok?"

"I guess so," Tom nods. "Got a couple swipes but no bites. I imagine they had to sew him up."

"Holy shit."

"Holy shit is right, my friend." Tom reaches for the gun and clutches the barrel. "That's where the gun comes in."

"Shouldn't you . . . or . . . someone have called someone?"

"Someone did call someone. They showed up with the ambulance and police cars and all that. Couple guys poking around the woods. One had a *dart* gun. Said they'd be back today and told us all to call them if we saw the bear. Useless." Tom's pupils are dilated: big black saucers in his eyes that give him a wild look.

"Why today?" I rub my temples.

"You look a little like shit," he says.

"Joey's coming today," I tell him. Joey, my son, and Jen, my ex, started driving from New Brunswick yesterday. They called last night from outside of Montreal and said they were going to leave as early as possible this morning, hoping to be here by early afternoon.

"For the summer?" he asks.

I nod.

"All the more reason . . ." He pulls the gun close to him, and I can't help but picture him in a bed, spooning it. "Better get yours loaded," he says. "'Be Prepared,' eh? Like back in the Boy Scouts."

"I don't have a gun, Tom. And I was never a Boy Scout."

"You don't have a gun? Huh. Well, you can borrow one of mine if you want."

The idea of telling Jen that I'm borrowing a gun to protect our son from a marauding bear makes my temples throb even more than they already were. I'm hoping that Jen's been irresponsible and they got off late. But Jen is never irresponsible and is never late. She says it's because of her "impeccable upbringing." Like the suburban, Saturday-night-hockey, perfect-little-house kind of impeccable. The watch your father work, drink and smoke himself to death by fifty-five while your mother struggles to keep her shit together kind of impeccable.

"Well thanks, Tom, but I don't think that's necessary. It's not really your responsibility."

"You wanna wait for the useless bastards from the city to do something?" he snorts.

I sit and slump over. My back steps are uneven, and it's uncomfortable. I wish Jen had just flown Joey out like she did during March Break.

"This must be something, on top of you being out so late last night, eh?" Tom shakes his head.

"How do you even know that?"

"Oh, I haven't slept. Heard the cab drop you off."

I look over his shoulder and imagine the bear bounding through the woods, crashing through those trees, gathering speed as it nears. "You have any Aspirin, Tom? I've got a bit of a hangover."

"Nope. Swore off them a while back. I smoke medicinal marijuana now."

"Really?" I've never figured out the details of Tom's workers' comp and I suspect it's a scam, or has become one anyway. He worked in one of the production factories over in the industrial park. Depending on the number of beers he's drunk, the position varies from floor supervisor to machinist. He's never said how he injured himself.

He leans the gun back against my steps and jams his hand in his pocket. He pulls out a poorly rolled joint. It's bulbous and cocoon-like. Lumpy. "Wanna puff? Cure yer hangover." He pulls out a lighter and sparks it. "I'd ask if you mind, but doctor's orders."

I know it's one more thing that'll piss Jen off, but everything pisses Jen off, so I accept the joint when he passes it to me. It's been a while and it tastes great. We pass the joint back and forth while he tells me about the complicated application process to get his smoking "license." It's too much for me to follow. Eventually he crushes the roach under his slipper.

"I'll be right back." He shifts over to his steps and grabs the rail. "I'll leave my gun, just in case." He pulls himself up and toward his backdoor, and I eye the gun knowing that even if the bear came into the yard I wouldn't be able to shoot it. I've never shot a gun before.

There's just a small wooden wall separating my place from Tom's, which is a mirror image of my house. There's a whole strip of places like ours on this side of the street. It's quiet, I'll give it that, but the only reason I live here is because Jen said my apartment downtown wasn't appropriate for our son. She had a whole list: Joey's bedroom was too small and had no windows. The place was too old. It was mouldy. There was a problem with the water pressure. The floors were creaky and splintered in parts and it got too hot in the summer, not enough natural light, young neighbours, busy downtown artery. Art spaces. Pawn shops. It went on. Now I'm here, and I know I'll never really fit in. I'll never be a Tom Fisher, and I'll certainly never be one of those guys with a garden who buzzes around on a riding mower, sipping hard lemonades and waving to the neighbours.

"If the pot hasn't cured your hangover, have one a these." Tom lets his screen door fall shut behind him and shambles down his steps. He's carrying two bottles of beer. I can see the drops of condensation on the outside of them. They look cold. They look delicious.

"Little early?"

He shrugs. "It's actually pretty late if you've been up all night." He hands me the bottle and plops down beside me. "So, Joey's coming, eh?"

"Yup." I crack the beer. The smell hits me. It's good. I'll have one, and then head back in to finish tidying the place. I remember I still need to set up the spare room too.

"If you don't mind me asking, how did someone so young come to be divorced *and* the father of a twelve-year-old?"

"High school," I say as though that's enough. I've never had a real conversation with Tom before and wonder how much he'll remember. "She was hot, but like, mature. Smart, you know?" I don't know what else to say because I never really felt like I understood her. "We just got together at a party one night, drunk, and . . ." I try to think back and find some kind of logic to things, but there wasn't any. "She got pregnant and I guess we decided to give it a go." I take a drink. Jen's still hot. She stays in shape. Dresses well. I take a bigger gulp of the beer. It's cold. Ice cold. At this moment, it could be the best thing I've ever tasted.

"You were both pretty young," he says, staring off into the woods, the beer bottle dangling between his spread knees.

"And what's your story, Tom? Why *aren't* you divorced? Isn't that the way it works these days?"

He doesn't look at me. There is actually quite a pause, and I don't think he's even heard me. Perhaps it's better this way. I'm not interested in Tom's marital advice, and certainly not in his marital life. So I follow his gaze back toward the woods, drink steadily and stare. There's movement every so often, a swinging branch, rustling leaves. I think about the Dahl boy, but the only image that comes to mind is one of gaping wounds and a small body doused in blood.

I imagine the bear bursting through the brush and lunging into my yard.

"I don't know," he says suddenly.

"Sorry?"

"I don't know why we aren't divorced." He puts a hand down beside his leg and pushes off to stand. "Finish 'er up. Time for round two." I'm not even half done my first, but part of me wonders if he'll even come back, or if, somehow, I've offended him.

About midway through the third beer there's a lull in the conversation. I've grown thoughtful. Tom, I notice, has simply fallen asleep. His head is leaning against the railing on his steps, his mouth slightly agape, a little spittle forming at the side. He's breathing heavily, erratically even. I glance up at the sun. It's moved directly overhead. I listen to the sounds of the burbs: the rat-a-tat-tat of a sprinkler, two dogs barking at one another across fenced-in yards, cars gliding slowly down the street and, finally, the sound of a car pulling into my driveway. The sound of one, and then two doors closing.

They're here.

Dropping my bottle at the bottom of my steps, I stand. I've got to hope that Jen doesn't come out here. I've also got to hope that Tom doesn't suddenly wake up and come stumbling into my house, gun in hand, rambling on about bears. I rush into the house and through the kitchen. I take a quick scan around the living room. There are albums, magazines, video games, dishes, takeout containers and a few changes of clothes lying around. There's a garden hose under the coffee table.

I open the front door and see them standing in the driveway, stretching off the long drive, yawning and staring up into the sun. Joey has grown visibly larger in only a few months. His arms look awkwardly long; his legs have thickened. His hair is shaggy and hangs in his eyes. When he sees me standing on the steps, he hesitates, but then he strolls over toward the house. He's developing the kind of swagger that I see other teens affect at the mall. He looks good. He looks like a normal kid. My normal kid. I grab him and hear a "Hey, Dad" from my chest. I kiss the top of his head and smell generic, hotel shampoo. Jen is standing with her arms folded over her chest. She does look hot. I imagine she does herself up for me. She probably wants to look her best. Isn't that something chicks do to their exes?

I would love to just wave and have her be on her way, take Joey in and get some records on. Find out what he's listening to these days. "Hey Jen, you look great," I say, and try to keep my voice steady. Joey pulls away and walks behind me.

"You look awful," she says and leans in for a brief hug.

"How was the drive?" I ask as she pulls away, but I can see that something has changed. That resigned look is gone. She looks over my shoulder at our son.

"Joey, can you go to the car for a few minutes."

"Why's the hose in the living room?" He's already half in the front door.

"Now, Joey," she says.

Head down, he turns and walks toward the car.

"Have you been drinking?" She doesn't separate her teeth when she speaks; it's like a hiss.

"No, no . . . Listen, last night, I . . ."

"Have you been drinking today? This morning?" There's a certain finality in her tone this time.

"Jen, look . . . Yes. Yes, I have. Just one with Tom, the neighbour. He's having a rough time."

"Your son is coming to stay with you for the summer, and you couldn't stop drinking for one morning?" Her eyes are huge, bulging on her face, and I can see the strain on her lips from trying to keep her voice down. We've promised not to fight in front of him anymore.

"Jen, you don't understand," I begin, but I can feel it now, the beer. It's hitting me hard now that I am standing in the sun, dehydrated and exhausted. "It was nothing." I have to try not to sway, to keep my voice even.

"You look like shit. Like absolute shit. You look like you were you out all night. Have you slept at all?" She's bursting. "Do you know how much he's been looking forward to this?"

I look over her shoulder and see Joey standing by her car. He won't look up at us. He's got his hands crammed into the pockets of his shorts and he's kicking the side of the tire. Over and over again he kicks it. Why couldn't she have just flown him out like on March Break?

I don't even notice that she's begun to walk away.

"Hey . . ." I begin, but she just glares back at me quickly. Joey watches his mother. She's telling him something. His face contorts, and he says something back. I can see their mouths move. I can hear the sound of their voices, but it's only noise to me. They get in the car and begin to drive up the street. I feel like I should say something; that I should yell. But I don't. I just stand there and stare at them, first imagining and then wishing for the bear to come back. Willing it to rush out from behind the house and throw me to the ground, maul me with its massive claws and then drag me back into the forest.

MY SUMMER WITH SETH

Hey,

I saw you the other day in the London Drugs on Yates and Quadra. I saw you and followed you around the store. Seeing you there got me to thinking about that summer: the summer just before I arrived in Victoria and we met. I should have told you the truth about it when we were still together. I guess it just became one of those things. I liked the mystery that built up around it. How you called it The Lost Summer and made things up about it.

"Robbing banks across the American Midwest?" you'd ask. "Hefting massive satchels of marijuana through tunnels under the BC–Washington border? Fucking prostitutes in South East Asia?" I remember once, you returned home from work, barged into the living room and without any preamble declared, "You must have been harvesting abalone off the west coast of Australia!" because you'd just read an article about it.

I shook my head. "Nice try, babe," I said, and you just stood there tapping your toe and giving me that look of yours – eyes squinting, head tilting, lip rising in an almost-sneer – I call it your you-bastard look, and I loved it because it was so cartoonish. You gave it to the cat all the time when he sprayed the apartment or shit outside the litter box. I saw you give it to people in public too, when they cut in front of you or blew cigarette smoke in your face.

Maybe after all of that, I thought you'd be disappointed with the truth. Because maybe the truth is nothing at all happened. Or maybe the truth is so strange that it's impossible to believe.

You knew the basics:
- I'd just graduated from high school
- I had a thirty-day VIA rail pass
- I had 1500 bucks to my name

I will promise you that I got on the train in Halifax that June with only the vaguest idea of what I would do. I had a hard time seeing more than a week into the future.

You could still smoke in the lounge car of the train back then, so I sat there because that was where all the hippies and bums sat; all the hard-luck middle-aged women; the tough-looking men with massive fingers on leathery hands that were stained black at every crease and always seemed to tremble a bit. I figured if I just stayed in my assigned seat, I'd never meet anyone. So I sat there even though I didn't smoke.

Seth Rogen walked into the car as we were cutting across the marshes on the border of Nova Scotia and New Brunswick. He was in his early twenties, pudgy with reddish hair and splotchy freckles. He had a Scrabble game under his arm and a cigarette behind his ear. He wore cargo shorts and an old worn T-shirt with an image of the Green Hornet on it, and he strutted through that car with confidence, joking with everybody, it didn't matter who.

Okay, it wasn't Seth Rogen, no one knew who Seth Rogen was back then. But in my memory that guy's become Seth Rogen. Perhaps it was the hair or the shirt. I guess you've already guessed that this Seth is the reason for my obsession. And it is an obsession: I can admit that now. I've made advances though. The Green Hornet sheets wore away to nothing a few years ago. I've parted with the comic books.

So Seth Rogen sat down across from me. He opened up his box and declared that he was ready and willing to whoop anyone's ass at Scrabble! No one else was interested, but I said sure. I'd only played a few times, but I started well, managing C-A-L-U-M-N-Y on my third or fourth turn (for a double word score at that) and Seth's brow wrinkled. He pulled the cigarette out from behind his ear and lit it.

"Hmm . . ." he mumbled, "not so bad for a kid." He was only a few years older than me, but I guess he felt much older because he'd just graduated from university. "I know what the problem is!" he declared, and pulled a little bag of weed out of one of the pockets in his shorts. "You wait, kid, we'll get off in Moncton and have a puff. I play way better when I'm stoned," he said, and I could tell by the way he said it that he wasn't lying.

In Moncton, the best we could do for privacy was to walk to the end of the platform. We'd brought with us an Acadian girl who had boarded in Sackville. Younger than me, she had a blond ponytail high up on her head. She was tattooed (a tree running up her neck) and pierced (ears, nose and brow) and intimidating because she was so big-eyed and pretty. She had that particular Acadian look to her, like Alain Leblanc, you remember him? With his dark features and soft lines? She could have been his sister.

"I just brought a little baggie. I'm heading out west, right? Where all the primo shit is, so I didn't want to waste my money on this east coast crap," Seth explained as he lit the joint.

"Where are you going?" The pretty girl's name was Manon, which I was afraid to say because it sounded too French, and I didn't trust my accent. Seth just went ahead and pronounced it Man-on, like the opposite of Man-off.

"I'm headin' to Jasper to work for the summer. I don't know where Kato here is going."

Seth called me Kato right away, and I was too nervous to ask why.

I tried to look into her eyes and shrug, but I had to look away.

"Jasper, eh?" She said it with a barely contained sneer. There was something about Manon, perhaps the slightly darkened skin around her eyes or simply the way she smoked the joint – as though she'd done it many times before – that made me very, very intimidated. She knew something about life that I didn't know, I was certain of that. Something important.

"Fuck-ing centre of capitalism, that place." I liked the way her accent made her emphasise the *ing*. It made it sound dirtier.

"Are you kidding me?" Seth's eyes were all pools of glass now; a big stupid grin cut his face in two. "It's fuckin' party mecca is what it is!"

"It is a tourist trap; resort town; playground for rich Americans and Europeans."

"How old are you? Jesus." Seth looked dejected. His wall of good nature had taken a hit. "You gotta relax, Man-on."

"So where are you going?" I asked.

"This is a secret. I cannot tell you."

"Are you kidding!" Seth laughed a Seth Rogen laugh and a big puff of smoke billowed out around it.

"No, it is not a joke."

"You're a weird chick."

"There is *nothing* weird about you."

We stared at her, wondering if we were losing something in translation.

"Damn. Let's retreat, Kato, *ma-dam-mo-zel* is wrecking my buzz."

Despite her animosity she stuck with us when we went back inside, maybe because we were the only people close to her age. We sat in the smoking car and she scribbled in a journal while we played Scrabble. Seth was right about playing high. By Rogersville he'd turned the game around. By the time we got to the Miramichi, I was asking for a rematch that I knew I wouldn't win.

Northern Ontario came across as very beautiful for the first few hours. Trees, broken only by lakes. Then trees and lakes. And more lakes. A lot more trees. By the second day, the allure had worn off: the landscape, sleeping upright in those chairs, the lack of showers. By the time we got to Manitoba we were all happy for the flatness: the open spaces.

Early one morning, I was sitting in the observation deck of the dome car, sipping a coffee when Manon came up and sat next to me.

"Good morning, Kato," she said.

I hadn't yet been alone with her. I was almost frightened.

"Where are you going to?" she asked me.

I took a sip of my coffee. My rail pass allowed me to get off and on whenever I wanted. Although I'd expected to stop and explore, I hadn't yet gotten off the train except to stand at the end of platforms.

"Jasper, I guess. Maybe I'll see if I can get some work there."

"Meh." Her face contorted when she said it: lips crinkling into a sneer; eyebrows bending up like an accordion. I was sure it was something only French people could do. "You don't seem like the type."

"What type?"

She threw her head back toward the rest of the train, her little ponytail shuddering on the top of her head. "Like Green Hornet, there." I took a sip of my coffee because I didn't know what to say. "He is such a guy-guy."

"Where are you going?" I asked.

She stared at me hard. Like checking-me-out staring. "It's a secret," she finally said. "Can you keep a secret?"

I wanted to ask her why she was so willing to tell me a secret, but I just nodded.

"It's a commune."

"A commune?"

"Yes, a commune. Near Jasper."

"Why couldn't you tell us?"

"Because it's against the rules. And Green Hornet is not the type."

"I don't get your problem with him." I felt protective because he'd been so protective of me: taken me under his wing and led me through this trip.

"He is a frat boy wannabe."

He had gotten quite intoxicated the night before and had said some crude things, but I thought he'd been funny. The people in the lounge car certainly agreed.

"It's a very progressive community." She stared directly at me as she spoke.

"So why are you telling me?"

"We move around constantly to avoid the police and park wardens. It's a tent commune."

"Tents?"

She paused and considered me. "You are different. You are a thinker."

I blushed and felt like an idiot for it.

"I can see it. You like your friend there because he is so outgoing; he is like a natural leader. These are qualities that maybe you don't have."

"He's not that bad, really. He's super nice. He likes everyone. He likes you."

"He wants to fuck me." She drummed her fingers atop the table between us. I blushed again. "Guys like him are all over places like Jasper. They go there to party and have sex."

I was staring down at the plastic top of my coffee and when I looked up she was still staring at me. She stared until I had to look away.

"Stick with me, Kato." It was three in the afternoon and Seth Rogen was getting drunk. We'd just pulled out of Edmonton, on our final push to Jasper. "You stick with me and you'll have the summer of your life." We'd run out of pot somewhere near Unity, Saskatchewan, and Seth had started drinking to battle the boredom. "Last summer! Man, let me tell you! Last summer . . ." He took a drag of his cigarette. There were only a few other chain-smokers in the car at the time. "The parties, Kato! The ladies. Fine ladies in the mountains, right. Athletic types. Hard bodies." He finished his beer. "You got a lady, Kato?"

I shook my head. I hadn't had a real girlfriend since Shelly McPherson in the eleventh grade. She was my first time. We dated for eight months. I told you about her. She was the longest before you.

"All the better, my friend. Girls always get better staff housing too, so you gotta hook up with one to have a decent place to go." His face was red and splotchy, his cheeks huge with his perpetually smiling mouth.

Manon entered.

"Man-on! Come have a drink with us."

She sat down next to me.

"I'm gonna get us all a drink. Celebrate the occasion. Whaddya think?" He got up and went over to the canteen.

Manon spoke quickly, "You should come with me. Come and check it out."

"I don't know. It sounds cool, but I –"

"You what? What do you have to lose? You are taking the easy way with him. Go to Jasper and get a job filling hotel room mini-bars and drink away your paycheque every night. What will you learn?"

"Learn? What's anyone got to learn here?" Seth returned with three cans of beer, which he plopped down on the table. "Learning's for school." He cracked a beer and held it up for a toast. Manon and I did the same. "To fine companions on a fine journey!"

We clinked cans.

Manon put hers down and declared, "I have an offer."

"A what?"

"An offer. I have an offer for you two."

Seth sat back. "What kind of offer you got for us?" He winked at me.

"I'm offering to take you two with me."

"And where the hell are you going, exactly? I thought it was a secret."

"It is a secret. But I will tell you, it's a commune. In the mountains."

"A commune?" he almost yelled. "Like hippies and shit?"

Manon tossed her head back and forth. "I guess so. But we like to think of ourselves more like gypsies."

"Are you shitting me?" He looked at me but I couldn't look back. "Whaddya think, Kato? A new adventure?"

"It's a nomadic commune," she continued.

"Well how do we find this *nomadic* commune?"

"It is arranged already; *I'm* going to be found at the Jasper train station."

I wanted to go, but I didn't feel comfortable without Seth. I wasn't certain what had changed Manon's idea about him, but I was grateful. The idea of heading into

Jasper and getting a job seemed too fixed for me. Too much what I'd set out to avoid. So when Seth finally nodded and proclaimed that "this commune thing might just be kinda fun," I was relieved.

Manon glanced at me. I stared back and this time she was the one who looked away.

We got picked up in a biofuel-burning Volkswagen van driven by a dreadlocked stoner with dirty fingernails and dirt-black feet wrapped in crusty old Birkenstocks. His name was Leaf. He called Manon Lil' Tree, and she refused to respond to her real name from that point on. Seth took it all in good humour, immediately appreciative of the joint passed to him by Leaf.

"Here it is, Kato. The good shit," he said, his teeth clenched, not wanting to exhale.

Leaf pounded the van through some old logging roads for at least an hour and talked and talked, updating Lil' Tree on the changes since she'd left. She completely loosened up in the van: her ponytail, her facial features, the taut image of the tattoo that crept up her neck.

Eventually they began to tell us the history of the commune. There were about fifteen people in the group with two at a time out on operation (which meant gathering money and recruits). The leader was a guru named Now, who had reached a brief level of fame in the eighties after publishing a book on how to survive in the Rockies by communing with nature.

In all sincerity, Leaf said that the only rule of the commune was "to love thyself."

Leaf eventually pulled over and drove the van into a garage made of vines. We helped him wrap the vehicle in brush and then began to hike through a fairly dense forest. Seth grunted and stumbled along with his wheeled suitcase. It took about thirty minutes to get to camp. It was so well camouflaged and integrated with the landscape that it would have been easy to miss had you passed by just a few metres away. The roomy looking canvas tents were tucked under canopies of brush and blended well with the foliage. In a small clearing behind the main camp I saw a wood-framed greenhouse.

People exited the tents to greet us. There were lots of dreadlocks and dirty sundresses, dashikis and hiking boots. They all had odd names like Nature's Path and The Way The Moon Looks Tonight. Lil' Tree nudged me in the ribs when Now – a tall, gangly man – came out from a tent. He was barefoot, had a shaved head and was dressed in a pair of worn khakis and a baby blue button up. His lips were pinched into a tight grin and his eyebrows rose up on his forehead in rounded arches. When he approached, he put his hands together as though in a prayer and bowed slightly; he moved with such an air of serenity that it seemed as if he were floating.

He reached forward and caressed Lil' Tree's cheek with his thumb. He took each of our hands in his and rubbed. He had dainty, soft hands. Long probing fingers. "We've been expecting you," he said to Seth and me.

"Really?" Seth asked, sweaty now. Little bits of dirt and grime were stuck to many parts of his body.

"We shall call you the Hornet," he said to Seth.

"And you," he began, looking to me.

"Kato," Seth interrupted. "We call him Kato. A very powerful name."

Now continued, unfazed, "Kato it is." He closed his eyes and nodded. "Hornet, you shall join Leaf in the greenhouse. Kato, as befits your youth, you will join Lil' Tree in the school tent."

"But I just graduated," I blurted.

"As a teacher, Kato. You and Lil' Tree will be teachers."

She gave me a playful punch on the shoulder. Seth glanced at me with wide eyes and a big grin. He gave a little shrug.

We settled into the commune as quickly as possible, aided by the fact that the group immediately treated us as though we'd always been there. Hornet had some early success in the greenhouse and managed to remain perpetually stoned, which dried up any ambition to move on. As the new teachers, Lil' Tree and I replaced Mother II who left on an operation. We had only two students, Mousey (ten) and Bud (eight), and we taught them sitting around cross-legged in a tent. Our mandate, as described by Now, was to teach them absolutely everything we knew in any order at all as seemed most appropriate to the pupil and the alignment of the stars that month or something.

One day, it became obvious to Lil' Tree and me that the kids knew very little math. Or at least, seemed very wary of using it.

"Bud, how many years have both you and Mousey been alive?" I asked after they stumbled over some basic addition.

Bud just shrugged.

"What about 1+1, Bud?" Lil' Tree asked gently.

Bud looked down at the floor of the tent and turned over a small beetle that scampered in front of him.

"You know it's 2, right, Bud?"

Bud poked his finger at the beetle and let its scrambling legs tickle his fingertip.

"Mother II told us that 1+1 only equals 2 because Petrarky says so," Mousey said proudly.

Lil' Tree and I looked at one another. Petrarky?

"She says that the Man wants to hold us down with reason and logic."

"Patriarchy," I said, and Lil' Tree clasped her hand over her mouth. Her eyes danced.

Mousey nodded. "She says the world is way more complex than we can know, and that the only thing we can truly know is nature because we are a part of it."

Lil' Tree and I looked at each other. She told the boys the day's lesson was over. Bud gathered up the beetle and they ran from the tent.

"Oh God!" Lil' Tree cried, and we broke out in a fit of laughter.

"What do we do?" I eventually managed.

"I don't know. I think we should come up with a plan."

It was hot in the tent. I had begun to sweat.

"I can't even think about it now!" A tear slipped from her eye, and she sat in silence for a moment, shaking every so often with remnants of laughter.

"What made you change your mind about Hornet?" I'd been waiting to ask her this since we arrived.

She turned serious. "I decided you were valuable enough to take the risk with him."

"Why do you keep saying things like that? I'd be lost without him."

"No, Kato, you are better than him. A better person: sensitive. I saw it in your eyes, and now I see it in the way you are with the kids." She sat up on her knees and slid closer to me. "I am surprised he has lasted this long. He won't last the summer."

"How do you know I will?"

"I don't. I don't feel any certainty with you."

Her neck was red from the laughter and the heat. A vein had popped out and it seemed to pulse a bit under her tattoo. She stared at me like she had on the train the first time she told me about the commune.

"That is why with you, I feel there is a chance."

I felt myself blushing and hoped she thought it was the heat.

"You will see soon, Kato, that with Hornet, people are just playthings."

"But I'm Kato. The Green Hornet is nothing without Kato."

She shook her head almost imperceptibly. "You are more than Kato," she said and leaned forward. I couldn't move and watched her eyes close and felt her lips touch mine. Her tongue jabbed at my teeth. A long rivulet of sweat flowed down the side of my head and along my temple. I thought of Seth with his big goofy grin and his glassy eyes. The way he'd wrapped me in a bear hug when I finally beat him at a game of Scrabble. His stupid laugh.

I pulled back. Lil' Tree's eyes opened wide. I slipped out of the tent and walked away quickly.

I'd wanted to kiss her, I really did. But I just couldn't do it. It would have aligned me squarely with her, and I was not ready for that. I walked along a path that was just beyond the main fringe of the camp. Eventually I came upon the greenhouse. It was a simple, makeshift building; translucent plastic over a simple frame made from modified tent poles. They grew mostly marijuana in it, and a few other essential vegetables. The key was mobility. Everything had to be movable on short notice.

I approached from the rear and walked around it. The aroma of pot was intense. I noticed a thick haze of smoke hovering around the roof inside. As I came to the doors I saw Hornet and Leaf sitting at a small table in the middle. There was a Scrabble board on it. They were passing a huge joint between them. Even through the plastic and haze I could see their bloodshot eyes glowing red in the dense grey. There was an ease between them, a comfortable knowing. At one point, when Leaf said something that made them both laugh, Hornet reached over and grabbed his cheek and patted it; then he reached up and ruffled his hair. I knew Lil' Tree was wrong about him. He was never going to leave.

I turned and headed back to the camp. I passed a few people without acknowledging them, hoping I wouldn't run into Lil' Tree and lose my resolve. I went straight to my tent, grabbed my pack and crammed my belongings into it. I slung the bag over my shoulders and headed to the path that would lead me to the logging road. I would end up walking for five hours all the way to the highway, where I hitchhiked back to Jasper, caught the train and continued west to Vancouver. From there, I moved on to Victoria where I met you.

You know the rest; I don't need to go into details.

When I saw you in the London Drugs the other day you were with a guy, and I didn't want to know who it was, so I didn't say anything. I followed you two around though. Eventually you stopped and looked at vitamin supplements together, comparing them. At one point he said something and laughed. You gave him your you-bastard look, and I had to leave. I know it has been years, but seeing you there with that guy got me thinking about that summer and how we used to joke about it, and I wonder if I should have told you something about it. I wonder if things would have been different. If it would have changed things at all.

– Dave

FOOL'S PARADISE

The beach is packed today with sunbathers, readers, stand-up paddleboarders and the odd group of picnickers like us. We walked for almost half an hour along Toronto's western shores before we found a spot on this small grimy beach. It's hot. There are clouds in the sky, but they are cirrus clouds and as they pass in front of the sun they offer no protection from the heat. The only breeze is heavy, and it pushes the heat at us and wraps us in it before moving on.

Rosa loves the heat. In her slowly improving English she managed to tell me it reminds her of home. It's been a warm summer by our northern standards, but not for her. It being her first Canadian summer, she's having a hard time adjusting to the weather. She looks terribly beautiful today, and I can't help but stare at her sitting on a small pink towel with her legs bent at the knee and her smooth, dark skin glinting in the sun. Her head is tilted back to take it in. Her eyes close and lips part unconsciously to expose a hint of her white teeth. Her long black hair hangs over her arms. She is wearing a bikini, navy blue, and with her back arched, her small breasts point to the sun.

"John? John, did you hear that? Are you listening?"

"Sorry, what was that?" Sharon, my wife, is staring at me. There is a piece of cantaloupe in her hand. Its juices line her lips and drip down her chin. Her other hand rises to wipe it off her face.

"Alex was saying he's getting another promotion."

Alex shrugs. "I think I've got a good chance at becoming the director."

"Oh," I say, "that's great, Alex." I haven't been listening to their conversation.

Sharon's wearing a conservative one-piece, its bottom obscured by a purple sarong. Her large breasts threaten to pop out with every laugh, or every time she reaches into the cooler for a piece of fruit or a beer. They've gotten bigger over the years and hang off her chest like lifeless appendages. She still looks good, I guess, but she's got the type of body that looks spectacularly womanly when it's covered.

"I'm not concerned about whether or not I can do it. I know I can, I just wonder about the board. They almost know me too well." Alex sounds smugly modest. That's his way. He always manages a "but" somewhere in his dialogue even if left unspoken.

Alex received a scholarship out of high school, and I followed him to a small liberal arts university on the east coast. After graduation, I returned to Toronto with Sharon, and he'd gone travelling, completed a TESL course and ended up in Japan and Korea for a couple of years before moving on to Central America. Eventually, he came back here to work as a coordinator for this private language school downtown.

"They might want to inject some new blood into the school," he says.

"*Podríamos usar el dinero*," Rosa says right out of the blue. She's shifted now, moved onto her left side, laid out like some centrefold, legs on top of one another, thighs only barely touching. Her upper breast slips down her chest. I can see the darkening of her nipple and then the small piece of cloth settles into place.

"English, baby." Alex leans back and places a hand on her leg. He rubs her thigh in small, comforting circles.

She rolls her eyes. "Money. We can use the money." Alex knows enough Spanish that the two of them can communicate well, and she's been taking classes at Alex's school. I wonder what it is like for them at home, wonder if they do more fucking than talking anyway.

She reaches her hand up to tussle his hair, and he grabs it before it gets there and kisses it lightly. "Mucho dinero," he says and bites her finger.

We got to the beach at eleven a.m., hoping to beat the crowd. It's well past noon now, our picnic nibbled away. We've also had our fair share of beer, and I can tell both Sharon and Alex are feeling it.

"Been awhile since we did this, eh? Drank all day in the sun." He holds a sweaty bottle up to me. I raise mine back. Beer makes Alex nostalgic.

But it's true. When we lived back east, we'd spent more than a few days doing just this. But now it seems different. As the beer and heat work together to weigh down my brain, I think we do this because we feel as if we're still just young enough to get away with it.

I stare out over the water. Not even on a clear day can you see across Lake Ontario and in the haze even the horizon is obscured. But with a breakwater just off the shore coupled with the hovering seagulls, it's like we're on the coast – either of them – staring out over the vast ocean; not landlocked, peering south at the United States. Although I lived only briefly on the east coast, and harbour no strange connection to the ocean, this still seems like a cruel illusion.

Rosa has moved away from us and is lying on her stomach. A navy blue triangle of material does a gratefully inadequate job of covering her ass. Her arms are crossed, her head resting on them. Alex is sitting closest to her, his body obscuring my view of his fiancée.

Sharon has nuzzled up to me, slid under my arm and rested her head on my shoulder. "Mmm," she coos, "it's so nice here. I wish we could go swimming." Her hands run along my belly; her fingers tug lightly at the hairs there.

"You could," I say, staring out at the lake. It does look inviting. The water is very calm, lapping only a bit up onto the shore. People are in the water, especially down by the main beach, but we ended up far from there, near the Humber River, on a patch of sand overrun by a flock of haggard Canadian geese and surrounded by little cylinders of their green droppings.

"I remember us going swimming in the Bay of Fundy," Alex says. "I bet that water was freezing. I remember even you diving in," he nods to Sharon.

"That was different," she says.

"The only difference was we drank more," Alex points out.

"And we were covered in mud. And it was cleaner."

"Let's drink more," I say. Sharon's body is hot against mine. Her hair tickles the bottom of my chin.

The sun has cruised right on past us now. It's hitting mid-afternoon, the hottest point in the day. The beer is cool, though I notice we are running low. Rosa has stopped drinking, and Alex looks flushed from the heat and the alcohol.

"We should go down and check out the water," he says

"Oh, I so want to just dive right in." Sharon is nodding at Alex. She stands and begins to walk toward the water, staggering a bit. Her sarong has come off and I watch her ass shift under her suit as she walks away. She slips a finger under the band to adjust it. She's still got shapely hips though her ass has filled out, and she has scrawny ankles that are all out of proportion. She brings her hand up to mop the sweat off her brow and then bends abruptly, squatting like a child to inspect something on the ground. "Beach glass," she says, holding a piece of it up over her head. It is a large sliver of polished green glass.

Rosa moves up behind Alex, wraps her arms around his chest, leans her cheek against his back and whispers in his ear. Her eyes skim over the back of his head and meet with mine. I wonder what they're talking about. Whether or not she knows that Alex and Sharon have fucked. That he knows what that bare ass looks like; has probably clutched it in his hand while he moaned her name.

I must be getting drunk because I don't usually think about that anymore. It was before I even met Sharon. It shouldn't matter. Mostly, it doesn't. I reach into the cooler and pull out another bottle and some ice with it. I pick up my phone to distract myself, glance at my Facebook newsfeed, but I steal quick little glimpses of Rosa. My phone is warm in my hand, and it makes me think about the folder on my computer at home. The one full of downloaded porn of women who look just like her. How excited I was when one named Rosie ended up looking the most similar.

"I'm going down," Alex says, standing slowly, "fuck this heat." He walks down the beach toward Sharon who is standing at the water's edge. They say something to each other as they dip their toes into the water. There is a certain physical comfort among people who have had sex, and it makes me wonder if they still think about one another, remember the subtleties of each other's bodies, what it takes for the other to get off.

He shoves her toward the water, and she shrieks then laughs dramatically. It only comes up above her ankles, but she's jumping about and reaching for him, then pushing him. Alex is strong. Even when we lived together at university, I remember waking up and hearing him grunting every morning. I'd walk by his room and see him doing sit-ups or push-ups, and even now I bet he does the same. Seems like as soon as I got near thirty my body began to sag. I always said I'd start working out; do a few sit-ups in the morning; maybe take up jogging. It never lasted though. And fuck it really, what does it matter anymore? I'm Married. Getting old.

I lean back with another beer to watch Rosa, who has begun to twitch slightly as she dozes. I have done everything I can to imagine having sex with her. To have that lithe body wriggling under me or swarming over me. I take a large swig of beer and feel the condensation and the small pieces of ice melt off of it and drip onto my chest and it feels so cool, a single little drop weaving through my hair and down to my belly where it is dried up by the heat. I finish it with a second gulp and reach for another, the last.

Alex and Sharon are sitting, their knees pulled up to their chests, staring out over the lake. I can see the movements of their heads as they talk; see her head turn, and her lips move to explain something to him. I inch closer to Rosa. I can feel the sweat drip from my forehead, gather in my underarms and coast down my forearms. I pull my sunglasses off.

When I get next to her I glance over her barely covered breast. Finding women online with breasts as small as Rosa's has been the greatest challenge. You have to dig through amateur sites for that.

Rosa stirs a bit as my shape obscures the sun and places her face in the shadow of my body. I take a drink of beer, my upper body arching over hers, and a few drops of water fall down to her stomach. She flinches. I bring the bottle to her side. It moves closer and closer to her and then I glide it ever so lightly along the side of her stomach. Her chest heaves and I can hear her breath lurch from her mouth in a small gasp of surprise while both of her hands move quickly from her sides, her left going to where the condensation has fallen, her right up to shield the brightness from her eyes. And as her hand moves, her fingers graze my leg – the first time she has ever touched my bare flesh – and that piece of my leg comes alive. She pushes herself up, squinting into the sun and stares at me. I can see a little fear in her eyes and confusion and the motion of her body moving forward causes her hair to dance over her shoulders and settle there.

This is the part in the video when the woman usually acts surprised for a moment but then smiles and takes off her top.

"Sorry," I try not to slur. "You must be hot," I say stupidly because I can think of nothing else.

"No," she says quietly, and I can see her eyes travelling over me, the bottle in my hand, the excited rise and fall of my chest. She takes one quick glance down to the water where Sharon and Alex sit.

"Drink?" I raise the bottle to her. "It's cold."

She shakes her head and pulls her legs into her chest, her calves crushed against her thighs. Beads of sweat form where warm skin touches warm skin. Rosa is so close I can feel her warmth. I imagine I can smell the salty scent of her. I bring the bottle up to take another drink, but stop and move it toward her, keeping my eyes on her, and I let the bottle touch her thigh, run the smooth glass along her leg where it leaves a trail of dampness.

"Doesn't that feel good?" I ask, but her eyes squint, and she tilts her leg away.

"What're you doing?" she asks. She pulls herself tighter and once again looks back down the beach. "Don't," she says, and this time her voice has risen a notch.

My breath comes in short bursts, and I know I have to do something, grab her, or stand, or pour the bottle over my body.

She stands in front of me, and it is too much. Her body, hot, and glistening now with a sheen of sweat; her stomach and chest moving with excitement and fear and confusion. This is the part of the video where she is supposed to reach toward me, cup my groin and gasp at my erection, but Rosa just pulls away; I go to reach my free hand out to her but she flinches, so I pull back.

"Hey, hey," I lower my voice, soften it as best I can. "Calm down, Rosa. I'm sorry." I send a smile her way. She glares at me a moment longer, her eyes squinting and staring deep into mine, and then she turns and begins to walk down the beach.

Over her shoulder I can see that Sharon and Alex have stood again. He notices Rosa approaching and runs toward her. She screeches playfully as he gathers her up in his arms. She kicks and screams, writhes around in his arms so that the muscles on his back contract. He swings her around dangerously and then advances quickly toward the water. When he sets Rosa down, Sharon runs toward them laughing, and the two girls turn on him, each taking an arm, trying to push him toward the cold water. I can hear their laughter plainly, and Alex's weak pleas to stop. I can see both of them, their hands all over his body, pulling.

I have to look away, and when I do, there is a loud splash. Although I don't look back, I can still see them: the fake shock on Alex's face as he sits in the shallows, the cold water washing over his legs and stomach, the two women standing above him and blocking the sun, laughing.

THE TUTOR

When Sean Major watched someone take her own life, he didn't fully believe that it was real. He'd been directed to the website by The Doomer, an online friend of his who'd promised "de sikest shit ul eva c." So he followed the link to seemysuicide.org and a streaming video popped up. It was a girl, live on a webcam. A teenage girl, maybe sixteen or seventeen, sitting in a bland white-walled room. She was slightly overweight, puffy more than anything, soft. She had short, dark, curly hair. There was a dullness to her expression. Her brown eyes – maybe a little too far apart – stared straight ahead without any emotion at all.

For a while she just sat there on her bed. He kept expecting her to start taking off her clothes. He was used to watching girls on cams strip and masturbate, but she just sat there. Eventually, she got groggy. Her arms, which had been propped up on her knees, gave out. She caught herself and laid herself down on her side. She winced once, maybe twice, it was almost imperceptible. Then her eyes rolled shut, her eyelids fluttered and she appeared to stop breathing. A fluid of some kind ran out from between her lips; it was difficult to see.

He watched her lie there for five minutes. Ten. Then fifteen minutes before finally having to turn away. He felt like he wanted to vomit, so he went into the bathroom and stood over the toilet. He shoved his fingers into his mouth but couldn't get them past his tongue. They tasted like white bread and metal. Instead, he ran a bath and soaked in it for a long time.

The Peer Tutoring Centre was always busy. Sean hated the waiting. There were booths where he and his students could go for privacy – and he always insisted upon using them – but when he had to sit and wait for his next appointment in the centre itself, it was excruciating. Many people used the round communal tables in the front. So there were always people at them hunched over textbooks and notes. So many hushed voices. So many people staring.

He had a first-timer who was already five minutes late, which meant he had to sit at the counter on one of the stools and wait. He tried to avoid making eye contact with Evelyn, the director of the centre, but she was one of those people who didn't like silence. He thought about turning on his laptop, but he didn't yet feel comfortable enough around her to ignore her.

"Your first-timer is on academic probation." Evelyn was at that vague crossroads of middle age, where, to his young eyes, she looked anywhere from forty to fifty-five years old.

"Okay," he said. He knew all about students on academic probation and how they were forced to go to peer tutoring. He turned slightly on his stool and glanced down at his shoes. They were old, black dress shoes. He'd wanted new shoes for a long time but couldn't afford them. He'd only received one paycheque from the centre so far.

It had taken him a long time to get a job. He didn't interview well. At the beginning of summer, he'd even bombed an interview at the Tim Hortons down the street from the dorm. Most of the people working there were immigrants who could barely speak English, and he figured that if they could do it, so could he. The manager – a middle-aged man with bad acne scarring and thin, pale limbs – had conducted the interview. Sean's first thought was that the man was stupid, but when they sat down to do the interview, Sean couldn't speak; he found himself virtually incapable of giving anything more than one-word responses. The banal nature of the questions ("What do you see yourself bringing to the team here at Tim Hortons?") disturbed him; they made him think that the manager was put off by him, was convinced that Sean thought he was too good or too bright to work at the coffee shop. The manager was pulling a power trip because the only power he had was there; the only power he would ever have over Sean was in that interview. Sean began to sweat. He felt it on his forehead, right at the hairline. He felt it on his back, first dribbling then streaming right down into his pants. His glasses started to steam up. He tried to wipe his forehead inconspicuously but there was too much. His glasses slid down his nose and he let them rest there. He kept looking down at the brown-tiled floor, waiting for the pool to form. Waiting to be swept away. Swept along the spaces between the tiles on the floor and then flushed down into some drain.

"That's her there," Evelyn said, pointing at the door. "That's her. Samantha McKinnon."

She was standing at the doorway looking around, hand on her hip, annoyed. She was one in a sea of girls all over campus Sean found generically attractive. Blond, big eyed. First or second year, still with that roundness of youth, still tanned a deep brown from the summer. Her

T-shirt was too tight. It was white and had a pink star in the centre between her breasts. Even from that distance he could see the outline of her bra. She was wearing shorts, very short shorts. Her thighs were thick, her legs long, rounded.

He heard Evelyn's voice; he could register that she was still talking, but he couldn't listen. "She's a girl," he said.

"Sorry?" Evelyn tilted her head, stared at him.

Sean finally turned away from the girl and looked back at Evelyn. He swallowed. "I haven't yet, you know . . ."

"What?" Evelyn looked at him. She picked up the schedule, printed out on a clipboard. "Sorry?" she said again.

"Girl. I didn't know it was a girl." On the schedule it said Sam McKinnon: Computer basics.

Evelyn laughed. "There are lots of girls at the college. Some of them even come for tutoring."

He could sense Sam approaching from behind him and could imagine her staring at him. She was probably already judging him. Planning on how to humiliate him. She would be derisive during their sessions. She would be disgusted by him. She would stare at the pimple forming on his forehead. The slick greasiness of his skin. Sam would ridicule how out of shape he was. She would judge his shoes – especially his shoes – and she would rush off to mock him to her friends.

Then she was there beside him, and she was talking to Evelyn. He stared straight ahead.

"Hey, Sean." Sam reached out her hand.

"Sean, this is Sam," Evelyn said when he didn't move.

"Yeah. Um. Hi," he said and reached out his hand. He felt the wetness of his palm and noticed that his hand was the same size as hers. He didn't want her to look at his fingers. They were thin. They were thin and pointy and he knew his hands were the kind of hands that had never worked; that had never done anything but type on a keyboard.

"So you're gonna get me off AP?" She smiled at him. He had to look down. Her hand was at her side. Her fingers were folding into her palm to rub away his dampness.

"Here," he said and pointed to two seats at one of the round tables. There were two other sets of students at it. He couldn't be alone with her.

She went over toward the table and flung her backpack onto it. Sean followed and sat next to her. Her hair was shoulder-length, thin and very straight. Her bangs were cut at her eyebrows. He noticed her eyebrows were much darker. He tried not to, but he couldn't help think that was the colour of her pubic hair.

"Where do we start?" she asked, but he didn't hear her.

He had to jog across the parking lot to the dorm hunched over to hide his erection. He ran into the apartment and turned on his computer. He sat, his fingers drumming out a beat on the table beside his keyboard. He closed his eyes and all that he saw was Sam. Her legs. What it would feel like to sink his fingers into the thickness of her thigh.

When the computer was on he typed freefunfor-boys.com into his browser and went to the site. The daily uploads were listed at the top of the screen: three thumbnail teasers per row. He scanned them, then the next row. He scanned the tiny images of the girls, looking for just the right one.

He clicked on one and the video popped up. He undid his pants. He masturbated as the video played out, a simple scene with a girl and a guy on the couch. But it wasn't right. She wasn't right. Her hair was too long, too platinum. Her groin was shaved. She was too thin.

The next video he tried was closer. The girl was more athletic. She had the dyed blond hair; the bangs; a trimmed, dark V of pubic hair. She was in a kitchen and squatting in front of a man who leaned back against the counter. He was muscular, his cock so long and veiny that it made Sean uncomfortable, but he just focused on her. On the way her thighs stretched as she squatted, on her hand between her own legs, touching herself. He closed his eyes and sat back, listening to the video, the sloppy wetness of it, and imagined him and Sam in one of the private tutor booths. His hand was on her thigh, so white against her tanned skin, and she placed her hand over his.

She moved it up her leg. He could feel everything, the little blond hairs, every little ridge of muscle, every littler shiver. His fingers slid between her thighs, underneath the edge of her shorts. He felt the band of her underwear and slipped his finger under it. Sam moaned.

MajorMajor	Cant find it anymore. cmysuicide?
The Doomer	she made news. bigtime shit. Gonzo. theres other plases
MajorMajor	Where?
The Doomer	sitesnshit wer suiciders hangoutnchat
MajorMajor	About what
The Doomer	how y sending link
MajorMajor	Thanks. Hey, I met a girl
The Doomer	No one dose it onlin tho too risky
MajorMajor	Yeah it was wierd to c her do it
The Doomer	u met a girl. A camgirl lol
MajorMajor	No, a girl at school
The Doomer	i get off ondatshit
MajorMajor	Shes hot
The Doomer	the offinself stuff. watchin fat chick go wasfcked
MajorMajor	it made me feel wierd. I dont know how i feel
The Doomer	yer girl no u 2 met :)

MajorMajor	Funny. Yeah she knows
The Doomer	u love it
MajorMajor	The girl? The Fat chick?
The Doomer	Watchin her do it
MajorMajor	The suicider? Maybe
The Doomer	Im gonna pretnd toba suicider n talk to em
MajorMajor	Really? Why?
The Doomer	Itll b hilarys.
MajorMajor	Yea. Cool. I gotta go
The Doomer	gotta go b wit yer chik
MajorMajor	Lol. Sleep. school in am
The Doomer	so yul b wit her in yer dreams lol
MajorMajor	FU
The Doomer	Sweet wet dreems. Doomer out

"I can't think about stupid computers, I gotta write an essay."

"You're going to use a computer to write that essay."

"Whatever."

It was their third session, and she'd insisted that they go into a booth. He set up his laptop and tried to focus on the screen. Sam was wearing a skirt. A short, greyish skirt and one of those tank tops with thin straps.

"I'll cheat. I'll pull something off the Internet." She had her face glued to her iPhone. Now that they were alone, she was turning into the person he thought she would be: unresponsive, bored.

"You can't cheat," he said, glancing over at her. "You can't do that." He tried to look away, but he couldn't.

She crossed her legs, the skirt slipping up her thigh. "Sure I can. There are tons of essays and stuff online." Her finger slid across the screen of her iPhone.

"Teachers aren't that stupid." Sean wondered what she was looking at. Her tank top clung to her. He kept picturing himself sliding his finger down along the groove between her breasts, cupping them.

"I'll, like, change the words around and stuff." She puffed out her lips and blew air up her face, fluttering her bangs along her eyebrows. "The font."

"Teachers aren't that stupid," he said again.

"Some of them are," she said and finally looked up from the screen. She grinned a little grin, and Sean had to look away.

She could do anything she wanted, he knew. She could fuck her teachers to get anything she wanted. "I don't think they're *that* stupid."

She didn't respond, just refocused on her screen. He looked at the clock on his computer. It had been ten minutes already. "This really isn't hard, you know. I can teach it to you in twenty minutes. Everything you'll need to know to pass the test," he said. She was in the most basic of all computer classes: Documents for Admin Assistants.

A course devoted solely to learning the ins and outs of Word, Excel and PowerPoint.

"The essay is due in two days, and I haven't even picked a topic." She slid her iPhone along the table, uncrossed her legs and sat up. She smiled. "You could write it for me." She leaned forward, and Sean stared at the neckline of her shirt, wondering how far she'd go. How much he'd see. "Like instead of tutoring me, you could just write this stupid essay."

"What?" He could see her bra: the blue edges of it.

She dragged the chair forward, coming closer. He could smell her. Shampoo and sweat. Slightly pungent. She reached across the table, and he thought she was going to touch him, but she stopped there, tapped her fingers. Her fingers were long and looked strong. They looked older than the rest of her. Her nails were painted red, but they were chipped and growing out. The nail on her index finger was much shorter than the others. He imagined her hand slipping under the table and out of sight. Imagined her asking him what it would take to get him to write her essay. He could feel her long fingers moving up his thigh and then the palm of her hand pressing against him as she undid his pants. She reached in and pulled him out. He saw her long fingers stroking him slowly.

"Whaddya think?" She pulled her hand away from the table and sat back.

"Um," he started, but couldn't find the words. He could barely think. He looked at his computer screen. Focused on it, the blank Word document. "No," he said. "I could lose my job." He looked down at his shoes.

"You're not an English tutor anyway, right?" she said, slumping in her chair.

"Right," he said, although he knew the kind of essays she had to write for her composition class and could easily pump one out.

She grabbed her iPhone again and sat back. "You know, we don't have to do anything. You get paid whatever we do, right?"

He nodded, but she didn't even look up to acknowledge him.

"So, like, we can just sit here and you can sign my AP form and everything's fine." She was back to touching away at her screen.

Sean took a deep breath and closed his eyes. He appreciated the moment of silence. Then Sam giggled. "What're you looking at?" he asked.

"Nothing, just some stupid website."

"What website?" He touched the mouse pad and moved his cursor to Firefox and went online.

"You ever heard of hotterorfodder.com?"

He typed in the URL and the page came up. There was a lot of advertising for dating websites and a picture of a woman in the centre. "What is it?"

She shuffled over, dragging the chair up beside him. The scent of her again. "So these people are total losers, right. They upload their pictures and you vote on whether or not you think the photos are hot or if they should be dumped from the site. I guess it's been around forever."

Sam reached over toward the computer and her fingers touched Sean's. He pulled his hand out of the way quickly. He looked at the picture of the girl. She was young, early twenties, dressed mostly in black. She had on a T-shirt covered in black skulls with bow ties. Above the photo there was a list of flames of various sizes that represented the numbers one to ten.

"Gross. So emo," Sam said. She clicked the smallest fire, just a little spark amongst a pile of wood. "I guess she could be all right if she didn't hide under all that black shit." Sam was enthralled. He watched her go through a few of them, analyzing each one carefully before assigning a fire and moving on.

Eventually Sam noticed a sidebar ad for the new Kween video. Kween was some sixteen-year-old Aussie pop star who was the latest big thing. All Sean knew about her was that she dressed in elaborate costumes and made the kind of dance-pop music that all sounded the same to him. The world was pumping out pop stars faster than he could keep up. But he watched the video, fascinated. At one point, near the end, when the music had ramped up to a grinding, industrial peak, Kween appeared under a strobe light, her face painted like a skull, naked except for strategically placed pieces of black electrical tape. Other young girls made up similarly surrounded her, placed their hands all over her as she wailed.

"Oh my god, I've got an even better site!" She shoved herself over, directly in front of the laptop and began to type. She pushed her body against his. He could feel her hip nudging him. "Ewwww!" She shook in disgust and brought her hands up to her face, closed her eyes. She had a huge grin on her face.

He looked at the screen. There was a photo of a toilet bowl, a long brown piece of shit floated in yellow water. The top of the page said Rate My Poo.

"Hey, Sean," she said. "This is the best peer tutoring session ever." She gave the shit a ten and another popped up. He watched her feign disgust, but giggle and burn red. Her pupils danced, taking in every corner of the shot.

"Six," Sean said. "Six."

"Six? Why?" Sam looked at him.

He pointed at the screen, his finger resting just in front of it. He traced the outline of the piece of feces on the screen. "It looks like a six on its side," he said.

"Oh my god! You're totally right!" She burst out laughing and rated it. Another image popped up. Then another. It was endless.

The end of the session came too quickly.

"Hey," she said, slinging her bag over her shoulder.

"I'm heading over to the pub to get a drink with some friends. You in?"

Sean stared at her.

"So?" She stood there for a few moments at the door.

"I, um." He wanted to say yes. "I have another student," he said.

"So, come over after." She shifted the bag on her shoulder, her hand slipping under the strap. She shrugged. "Well, if you can make it." She turned. "Thanks for your help!" Sam laughed and exited the booth.

It was only four o'clock, and the bar was nearly empty. Sean had barely consumed alcohol in his life, and he'd never been in the campus bar. It was functional: slick concrete floors, plain brown tables, a pool table in one corner, a dartboard on the back wall. The only particular draw seemed to be a huge flat screen TV that was broadcasting sports highlights.

Sean only regretted his decision after he'd sat down at the table and been introduced to everyone. There was another girl named Parvati and three guys, but Sean forgot their names as soon as they were introduced. The guys reminded Sean of the jocks he went to high school with. They dressed in the same blue jeans and sports T-shirts. Sweaters with the school's name on it. They were usually zoned out on iPods, drifting through the halls with stunned expressions on their faces. Ball caps slightly askew. They didn't know what to make of Sean, and one guy in a Maple Leafs shirt spoke to him like he was a barely tolerated little brother, but they kept topping up his glass with beer from the pitcher. He forgot how alcohol hit him from behind the eyes first. A little hum there.

Sam and Parvati got up to use the bathroom. Sean didn't want to be alone with the guys, so he followed them. Sam was ahead of him, and he watched her turn into the hall where the bathrooms were. He turned the corner as the door swung shut. He imagined walking up to it, pushing it open and entering. Walking up to the stall Sam was in and knocking on it. He imagined opening it and pushing her up against the wall behind the toilet, sitting her down on the back of the toilet and kissing her, and it was wet and sloppy, and he shoved his tongue in her mouth so hard that her head knocked against the wall. He slid his hands up the sides of her legs, gathered her skirt up around her waist and then dragged her panties down her thighs. He knelt, hovering over the toilet beneath him and buried his face between her legs. She grabbed his hair in a bunch and pushed, squeezing her thighs together against his face.

Sean gathered water in his palms from the faucet. He splashed it over his face. There was a thud thud thud in his chest and his vision was blurred. He was so hard his erection pushed against his pants, rubbed, got harder. He tried to hide it but he couldn't. He walked toward a stall and the bathroom door swung open. Maple Leafs shirt walked in. Sean turned his body quickly.

"Hey Tutor," Maple Leafs shirt said, walking up to one of the urinals.

"Hey," Sean said and went into the stall. He sat down on the toilet seat and closed his eyes. He tried to think of anything but Sam. The guy out there holding his dick; his piss spraying against the back of the urinal. The guy washed his hands and exited. After a few more moments, Sean stood up and exited too.

When he got back to the table, the guys were silent. They wouldn't look at him. One of them, the biggest of the three, seemed on the verge of bursting. He brought his beer to his lips, but couldn't drink it. He finally started laughing and Maple Leafs shirt hit him in the shoulder. "Shut up," he said, but was smiling as he said it.

Sean kept his head down, but he could feel them looking at him.

"You gettin' off in the guy's washroom?" the bigger guy asked and the three of them finally stopped holding back.

"Where's your stiffy, dude? You have a little tug in there or what?"

Sean stood up, turned around and began to walk very quickly away from the table. He saw Sam and Parvati returning from the bathroom. He walked quicker.

"Hey, what's up?" He heard Sam ask. "Sean?" she yelled. Then he heard talking at the table, more laughter. "You can be such an asshole, Darius," Sam said loud enough for Sean to hear.

He was almost at the door. He could see it, the outside, and could feel the cool air on his burning skin. He heard Sam behind him saying his name again, but he kept going. He wanted to run, but couldn't bring himself to do it. He wanted to run all the way back to residence and lock himself in his room.

MajorMajor	When did you first think about it
LonelyGirl14	I don't know
MajorMajor	I was really young
LonelyGirl14	The bullying started in 7th grade
MajorMajor	Was that when
LonelyGirl14	It was probably then. I just turned 16 last month
MajorMajor	You seem so mature
LonelyGirl14	How old are you?
MajorMajor	19

LonelyGirl14   And you still think about it?

MajorMajor   No Im just waiting for the right time.

LonelyGirl14   So you know how and everything

MajorMajor   Of course dont you?

LonelyGirl14   I dont know. Moms got pills. She's got lots. How are you going to do it?

MajorMajor   Dont use pills. Pills r no good. Too risky. Might not work.

LonelyGirl14   I dont know then

MajorMajor   Then yer not too serious

LonelyGirl14   But I cant handle it anymore

MajorMajor   If you havent even thought of how . . . I havent even wondered in years. Ive known for a long time

LonelyGirl14   We have guns. My father has guns.

MajorMajor   Like shotguns?

LonelyGirl14   He hunts.

MajorMajor   Could you pull the trigger?

LonelyGirl14   I dont know

MajorMajor   Could you put it in your mouth and pull the trigger?

LonelyGirl14   Is that the best way?

MajorMajor   Make sure its pointed straight up so it goes through the brain

LonelyGirl14   How are you going to do it?

MajorMajor   I have a gun right here

LonelyGirl14	Your doing it tonight?
MajorMajor	I cant wait any more. I cant do it. Its too hard. Its all too hard.
MajorMajor	It's the best revenge.
LonelyGirl14	It'll destroy them, right? The fuckin assholes
MajorMajor	Completely. Completely

Sean lay in the bath for a long time. It was hot, and when he first got in he watched the steam rise off of his pale skin. He tried to masturbate, but his penis just lay limp against his thigh. He could think only about Lonely-Girl14. It was so easy to talk to her. She was just open and raw and waiting for someone to talk to her. Lead her. He wondered how she'd gotten to the point she had? It excited him, just a bit, to think of the strength of her desire to end her own life. How much emotional energy that must take.

He tried to picture her, but he couldn't. He wanted to picture her in her home, perhaps in her parents' bedroom – for effect – a conservative bedroom: a few family photos, matching dresser and bedside tables, floral bedspread. She would be dressed in black, right down to the painted fingernails. She had on big, black boots, army boots even. She was pale, he imagined, so pale that she seemed to verge on a bluish translucence. He could see the barrel of the gun in her hands, massive and thick, the butt of it resting on the ground between her legs. He could get right up to her neck and that was it. Was she crying? Was she pissed off? Was she beyond all that and just vacant?

He could picture her positioning the gun, reaching down and slipping her thumb over the trigger. He could see it engage and could hear the blast and smell the residue of the shot. There was blood and matter spattered over the bedspread, but he still couldn't see the face that the bullet had destroyed.

Sean was in the booth waiting before Sam even got there. He sat very patiently and tried to remain calm. He played Pac-Man on an online arcade simulator. Between levels four and five he took off his glasses and cleaned them.

At the time she was supposed to arrive he set up Microsoft Word. Today was the day they got down to business. Her test was so simple it was laughable to him. Mastering the basics of a word processing program. That was it.

She rushed in five minutes late. She stood in the doorway, her bag hanging from her hand at her side. She was wearing black tights and a T-shirt that hung down over her thighs. Black flats. She stood there and stared at him. "Hey," she said.

Sean glanced at her only briefly. "You're late," he said, and adjusted himself in his chair. He'd set up another beside him. "I have Word open, we should get started." He stared at the screen. The white space of a fresh document.

"Um. Right. Okay," she said and walked over to the seat. She sat down.

"You should take notes. I'm going to go quickly. You should know all of this stuff by now."

"Okay." She took out a notebook and a pen. She listened intently as Sean began his tutorial. He spoke quickly, moved the cursor around the program rapidly, clicking here and there. He could see her taking notes out of his peripheral vision.

"Hey! Did you get new shoes?" Sam dropped her pen down on the table.

"You've got to pay attention." He didn't look away from the screen, but he tucked his feet under his chair. He'd gone to the mall the other day. Gone to a shoe store in there that he would never even have considered going to before. It was small and sparse and the women who worked there were so attentive and attractive, but attractive like mannequins were attractive – all done up and machine-like. They were less intimidating for their automation.

He continued, moving into formatting styles. Sam was shifting in her chair. Folding and unfolding her legs – he could hear the fabric of the tights rubbing; tapping her pen against her notebook. She brought a finger from her free hand up to her mouth and began to chew on the nail.

"Sean," she said, her finger still in her mouth.

"If you're building a report document," he continued, "you might want to choose from one of the heading styles. During the test you'll probably be . . ."

"Sean," she said again, "I'm really sorry about the other day."

He stopped. His hand slid away from the touchpad.

"I don't know what happened, okay, and whatever, it doesn't matter." She reached over and touched his shoulder. Rested her hand there. "Darius can be an asshole sometimes. He was drinking . . ."

Sean turned his head just enough to see her hand on his shoulder. The way she gripped it, and just a little of the fabric bunched up between her fingers. He looked over toward her face. She was frowning, her head tilted. He thought that maybe this was the first time she wasn't wearing lipstick, so her lips looked paler, but softer. He was certain he could imagine what they felt like. He could see her tongue, twisting and turning in his mouth. She would grab him, he knew, with those long fingers. She would grab him and pull him to her. She would lie right down on this table and pull him onto her. He wouldn't let his lips come away from hers, his tongue leave her mouth. Her tights rolled easily down her thighs. She undid his pants, pulled him out. He couldn't wait and thrust himself forward and into her, so easily. He could feel her squeezing around him. Her legs wrapped around his waist and she was squealing under his lips, his mouth pressed hard against hers, not letting the sound escape.

"Are you all right?" Sam pulled her hand away from Sean's shoulder.

Sean looked her in the eye. She looked concerned, still frowning. She didn't have much makeup on at all, and Sean thought that she looked amazing. More amazing than usual.

"I like you just the way you are," he said.

"What?"

Sean turned fully to his right and leaned toward Sam. Nothing registered on her face. She tilted back her head but didn't seem to understand what he was doing. He reached forward with his left hand and grabbed her shoulder. In one motion he pulled her forward in her chair. His right hand grabbed at her knee, thigh, slid in between her legs and felt her through the thinness of the material.

Sam tried to scream, but he crushed his mouth against hers, eyes open and watching her face. He pressed against her and she squirmed against his rough hand, digging fingers. She brought her hands up between them and knocked his arm off her shoulder. Her eyes jumped open, and she stopped trying to scream. She brought her other arm up between them and pushed him so that he fell away from her, rocking on the back legs of his chair. Her lips curled up in a snarl, her eyebrows crushed into her face, and there was a brief moment when he stared straight into her eyes and saw that her pupils had become black and empty, and then she brought both hands up in front of her, palms out, and slammed them into his face.

There was a great blast of light, and then sparks like static in a dark room. There was a terribly sharp pain and then nothing. He could feel the odd sensation of his blood trickling down the edges of his cheeks, up under his ears before dripping away. She stood over him. Her face was blotchy, red and contorted. She was straining not to rear back and kick him or kneel down and punch him in the face again. She said something – Sean could see her lips move – but he couldn't hear her, and then she turned around and disappeared from his line of vision.

He stared up at the fluorescent fixture on the ceiling. His eyes swam with tears and the stinging shock of the blow to the nose. A sharp pain gathered in the centre of his stomach. A sharp pain that radiated out, turning slowly. He rolled over onto his side, the acid taste of blood at the back of his throat, and vomited onto the carpet. His eyes continued to water, and then tears blurred his vision. He began to see a face in the blur. Glasses. Thin, black hair. He closed his eyes tight to squeeze out the water, but he didn't open them because the face became clearer. It was a girl's face, thin and pale. Big brown eyes, rimmed in black – makeup and the lack of sleep – big full lips, painted red.

She rested her chin on the barrel of a gun. He could finally see her face, so he held the vision for as long as he could. He studied her image for as long as it remained.

THE WRONG NUMBERS

When it occurs to me that I might be having a heart attack, my first thoughts are not of my childhood; they are not of my wife or family. I do not think, "I'm only thirty-eight, why now?" My life does not flash before my eyes. Oddly enough, the first thing that comes to mind is that I'm going to miss my mother-in-law's Thanksgiving turkey on the weekend.

It's an odd thought, I think, as far as last thoughts go.

I'm on the bus, on my way home from work, and I clutch my chest, sit up straight and look around for help. I can feel the fluttering of my heart in my hand. It's vibrating right through my flesh. I pull open my coat and notice my phone in my pocket. I'd set it to vibrate during a meeting this morning.

An old woman sitting directly across from me glares like I'm someone to be watched. She's all done up in that way old ladies get done up for the mall. She's curled her thinning, white hair and is wearing pressed pants with a nice shirt (pink stripes on baby blue). She's got a newish jacket folded over her lap; a modest shade of lipstick that has bled into the wrinkles above her lips. She must be in her seventies. I can imagine her as a beautiful young woman, as the object of someone's desire.

I pull out my phone but don't recognize the number. "Hello?"

"Yeah, hey. I'm calling about the apartment." It's a male voice; a slight, unplaceable European accent.

"Sorry?"

"The apartment, I'm calling about the one bedroom," he says again.

"You must have the wrong number."

"Oh yeah?" There's a pause, as though he's waiting for something else.

"Yeah," I finally say, "sorry."

He hangs up. Almost immediately the phone vibrates again.

"Hey, I'm calling about the apartment." The same guy.

"Sorry, wrong number. You just called."

"Is this 416-114-1976?"

"Yes," I say.

"And you don't know anything about an apartment for rent?"

"No, I don't. Sorry."

He hangs up again. I feel bad, but I don't know why. I slip the phone back into my pocket then put my hand to my chest. I leave it there for a moment until I can feel the faint pulsing of my heart.

Sandra's not home when I get there. I walk into the kitchen and see that she's got dinner prepped and ready to go: the cooked penne is clumping in a colander in the sink; there are chopped veggies on the cutting board; a jar of pesto and a container of parmesan sit on the counter. I check the oven: French bread.

I pull a bottle of red wine down from the small rack above the fridge, uncork it and pour myself a glass. It's not normal that she isn't home, but things haven't been normal since September when Sandra started her grad degree. It was around this time last year when she told me she wanted to do it. We were at our favourite Vietnamese place.

"Tim," she said, "I need a change. I need to do something." It came out like a sigh, like a secret she'd been harbouring for a long time and finally had the courage to say. "I want to go back to school."

"Oh." I was relieved. "Of course."

"That's it? *Of course.*"

I shrugged. "Why not?"

She looked down at her bowl of pho, disappointed. "It'll change our lives a lot. One income."

"Why now?" I asked. She'd been a social worker, in child protection. She'd never liked her job that much, but it hadn't seemed like the kind of job that people actually liked.

"If not now, then when?" She burned red. She'd been prepared for a fight. I reached over and touched the back of her hand with my finger. "We probably won't be able to go down south for the next couple of winters."

"Maybe we can," I said, and at the time, I thought perhaps we could.

"I want to do it," she said, "so that I can finally get out of child protection. It breaks my heart doing what I do."

I think back to her first apprehension, when she was just barely out of university, and how she had to come home before going back to the office. She had the baby in a car seat that she brought in with her, and there was a police officer there as well who had the stone-faced patience of someone who had done this before. She rushed in, put the baby down and fell into my arms sobbing. The officer stood by the door silently and waited, on guard.

🌀

She gets home when I'm halfway through my second glass of wine. She's got a flush to her cheeks and looks flustered. Her long, black hair is tied up on her head. She's wearing compression leggings that cling to her thighs; they make her look more muscular than she is. Her sweatshirt is loose and slips down her right arm, showing the strap of her blue sports bra.

"What are you doing home?" she asks.

"I came home early. Where were you?"

She brushes her cheek along mine, a short kiss near my temple. Her cheek is cool.

"Into the wine, eh?" She taps the side of my glass with her fingernail.

"Why not?"

"Why not," she says and grabs my glass and downs it.

When we go to bed I see that I've missed three calls on my cellphone. There are two messages.

"I'm calling about the apartment. My name is Angela. Please call me back tomorrow. Thanks." She left her number. I delete the message, and as soon as the next one begins "I'm calling about . . ." I delete it too. I turn to tell Sandra about the calls for the apartment, but she has already fallen asleep. I sigh too loudly, hoping to wake her. She doesn't stir, and I even watch as her mouth falls open and her eyelids shudder. I head to the bathroom to masturbate. I think about Sandra while I do it. Maybe that's a sign of aging, thinking about your wife while you jerk off. There's pasta sauce on her breasts; nipples salted with parmesan.

I'm sitting in my cubicle when my cellphone rings. This is the third one today, and it's not even noon. I take off my headset and answer it.

"Hi, I'm calling about the apartment." A young woman. "Hello?" She's got a nice voice; it's steady, smooth. Feminine.

"Sorry," I say.

"I was just wondering if it's still available. The one bedroom. I called and left a message last night."

There is a particular youthful quality to her voice: no hardness or edge yet. Nothing tarnished. It makes me want to listen to her.

"Hello?"

"How did you get this number?" My hand is shaking.

"It was on the website. Is this a bad time?"

"No, no, it's fine." My heart is beating quickly. "It's Angela, right?" I ask, remembering her voice from the night before.

"You think I could take a look at the one bedroom?" she asks.

"Do you mind if I ask you a few questions?" I take a deep breath.

"I'm not even really sure that I'm interested –"

"Is it just you? Alone, I mean."

"Oh, right, yeah. No pets, either."

"Good." I grab a pen and paper and begin to jot down notes. "Your employment?"

"Well, actually, I'm a student. Is that a problem? I'm a hostess at a restaurant on the weekends."

"Which restaurant?"

"Francesca's. You know it?"

It's in Little Italy and Sandra and I have been there a few times. I try to think about the hostesses, but nothing comes to mind. They are all attractive, I assume. Hostesses are always attractive.

"What do you study?"

"Sociology. At U of T."

"Are you single?"

"Excuse me?" Her tone tightens. "This is a lot of information."

"It's just that . . . it's just that the last tenant was engaged to this jerk and . . ." A bead of sweat slides into my eye. It burns. "The police had to be called." I rub it away.

"Oh. I'm single. Right now. I'm single." Her voice cracks. "Jesus." A big exhale.

"I'm sorry. You're right. That's too personal," I say.

"No, no. It's fine. I just broke up with my boyfriend. That's why I'm looking for a place."

"Wow. I. Oh, so sorry."

"He's not a jerk though. Like violent or anything. You won't need to call the cops."

"Okay. Right. Good. Thanks."

Silence.

"So can I see the place?" All of a sudden she sounds tired.

"Yeah, sure. Yes."

She asks when, and I mention this evening, right after work. Then I have to think fast.

"Can I just confirm that you have the right address? I manage a few places."

She reads the address back to me. It's across town, but not too far out of the way.

I arrive earlier than I expected and wait in my car. The apartment is in a small building in a residential area in the west end. It looks more than adequate for a young student living alone. I wonder if her parents are paying for it.

I ate too much at lunch and have to undo my belt a notch as I sit in the car. The other day Sandra mentioned that I was putting on weight. I told her that it was my winter insulation. She pinched the fat above my hips. "You'll definitely be warm this winter," she said and laughed. We used to go for walks, but then Sandra started going to a gym about eight months ago; she has a personal trainer and uses all those machines they have. I don't like to walk alone.

Angela is about ten minutes late, but I know who she is as soon as she turns the corner, eyeing the numbers on the buildings. She's East Asian, and I wasn't expecting that. She's wearing skinny blue jeans, a big wool sweater and has a large reddish purse over her shoulder. She's attractive in an undergrad kind of way. Her flesh still looks young; her face is full and round and a small chin protrudes. Long, straight black hair hangs in crisp folds over the bulk of her sweater. She finds the right address at the moment my phone rings. I check the number: Sandra

"Mom wants to know if we can pick up a couple bottles of wine for Thanksgiving dinner," she says without even a hello.

"Sure. Of course." I watch Angela take a quick look around the building.

"I figure two is fine. I'm sure they're already well stocked."

The girl walks up the few steps and tries the door, but it's locked.

"So you're okay with that?" I can hear the sounds of Sandra cooking: a spoon tapping the side of a pot. "Where are you anyway?" she asks.

"Yeah, fine," I say. Angela's reading the names on a board beside the door. It looks like she's about to push one, but then stops and takes a look around. She looks right at me in my car.

"Maybe you could grab some now? So we don't have to worry tomorrow."

"Yup. I'm driving. I shouldn't be talking. I'll be home soon."

Angela is staring at me. She takes a step down, squinting. I keep the phone to my ear. Now that she is staring right at me, I see that she is attractive. Beautiful even.

I put down the phone and start the car. Angela turns back to the building and pushes a button on the board. As I pull away I wonder if I'm beginning to think that all women are beautiful.

"No one drinks red wine with turkey."

"I thought maybe before. Or after." I bought a bottle each of red and white. Sandra's just noticed now that we are in the car and on our way north to her parents' house at the lake.

"God. Hopefully they have a bottle too." She sits far

back in the seat. She looks tired. She was at the library till late doing research. "I'm glad Jim isn't here this year," she mumbles. Jim is her younger brother.

"I'm glad the *kids* aren't here," I say. Traffic is moving slowly: the Thanksgiving exodus out of the city.

"That's what I meant," she says.

Jim and his wife have three kids. They live in Winnipeg and only make it home for Thanksgiving every two or three years. Last year the kids were four, seven and nine. It was exhausting because Jim and his wife pawned babysitting responsibility off on us. As I would have, I'm sure.

"I'm not looking forward to winter. Why doesn't winter get any easier as you get older?" She brings her right knee up to her chest. Her shoe is on the seat. It leaves a mark of dust.

"You think we can swing a trip down south this year? Maybe Cuba? It's cheaper." We've been going down south almost every winter for a while. Different countries each year, but they might as well be the same when you go to those all-inclusives.

"I'm sick of those trips." Her cheek rests on her knee and she looks over at me. "They're not even trips; they're *vacations*. Remember how we said we'd never go on trips like that." She's almost pouting.

"Things change," I say. When we were younger we used to go backpacking for extended periods of time.

"But for a while there, we actually got more bold as we got older. Remember Vang Vieng?" By our early thirties we'd already done Europe and South America and moved on to Asia. Sandra was a fearless leader on those trips. Leading us through jungle hikes; city tours; long rides on overcrowded, dilapidated buses. She could communicate with people so well – it didn't matter the race or culture or language. She'd been good at getting her point across.

"That was stupid," I say. "We got more stupid as we got older." In Vang Vieng, Laos, we'd decided to smoke opium and ended up staggering around the forest in a dream state, lost for what seemed like hours.

"It wasn't stupid. Dangerous maybe." She shifts and rests her chin on her knee, stares up at the highway ahead. "There's a difference. And it was no more dangerous than dropping acid at that full moon party in Thailand, or getting on a random bus in Goa and ending up in the middle of nowhere." She looks sad as she says it. Sometimes memories, even happy ones, aren't good things to have.

"So, I don't understand. Are you saying we should go on vacation or shouldn't?"

"I'm saying our vacations suck, so I don't care if we don't." She's looking away from me, out the window, and I wonder what she's remembering, and if it's the good things like the double hammock in our tree house in Chile, or the weekend stay in a blissful Shinto temple in Japan.

I reach over and pat her thigh. I leave my hand there,

but she doesn't take it. I'm not sure how to reassure her because I'm not sure what she's unsure about.

When we pull in at the cottage, Sylvia, Sandra's mother, is already standing on the front steps. She's got a glass of red wine in her hand.

Sylvia is still an attractive woman. She's grown solid with her age and, despite a few lines in all the typical places, her face has retained the essence of its youth. Her hair, still dark, hangs down to her shoulders. She's wearing a long skirt and a shirt that isn't buttoned all the way to the top and I admire her cleavage. I've always thought that, physically, Sylvia is a future snapshot of Sandra, and I'm okay with that. I'm okay with how Sandra will turn out.

She smiles and raises her glass. Her teeth are already darkening with the wine. "Couldn't even wait for us to get here before you got started?"

"Relax, Sandra, it's a holiday." She kisses her daughter's cheeks and then grabs me in an awkward hug. I worry about wine sloshing down the back of my coat. "Hello, Timmy," she says and kisses my cheek. I can feel the dampness of her lips and the warmth of her breath against my skin. "Why don't you tell my daughter to lighten up?"

Sylvia and Mark's cottage is more like a home. They own a condo in the city but only ever spend winters there.

The cottage has a wide-open main room containing the living room, kitchen and dining area, centrepieced with a wall of windows that looks out over the lake. With furniture, they have a tendency for the gaudy: Victorian-like and imposing. Walls overfilled with paintings, pictures. Elaborate lamps with even more elaborate shades.

Mark enters from the back deck through the sliding doors. He hugs his daughter and nods my way. Sandra may look like her mother, but she's daddy's little girl, and she and her father share a similar temperament.

"Oh good! You brought another bottle of red!" Sylvia pulls our wine out of the brown paper bags and checks out the labels. "Can we open it now? Let's open it now."

"Why not?" Mark says too loudly. "Tim, interest you in a brewski?" He walks to a cooler that he has set next to the fridge.

The beer is cold. Bits of ice still cling to the label, and it sweats in the warm air of the room.

"So how's the insurance business?" he asks.

"Fine." We are standing at an island in the kitchen. I can hear Sandra and her mother talking about Sandra's thesis at the dining-room table.

"You sell to companies, right? Not individuals."

We have this conversation almost every time we speak about my work.

"Probably more secure a job, right?"

"Why? You know something we don't?"

"No, no. I just mean if shit ever went down. You know, economic collapse and whatnot. Selling insurance to companies is probably a safer thing to do."

"Would you just listen to the four of us!" Sylvia stands up and comes into the kitchen area. "Talking about work and school! The things we should be avoiding on the holidays." She opens the fridge and pulls out a plate of veggies and a dip, and slides them onto the counter. We all reach for something and stand in silence. Sandra walks over to the window to stare out over the lake. I take too many sips of my beer, and eat four slivers of red pepper.

"I see your hair is starting to thin, Tim."

"Mom!" Sandra from the window.

"What? Sorry? Is it something you're embarrassed about?"

I can feel myself turning red, "Um, no, no. Not really."

"Oh yeah," Mark says, leaning in and squinting at my head.

"It's nothing to be embarrassed about, Tim, you're almost forty. I'm sure you've got a good few years left yet."

"Jesus, Mom. Are you drunk already?" Sandra moves toward us.

"Sandra, watch your language."

"You know, Tim," Mark begins, "it happens to the best of us." He puts his hand on his hips and bends forward as far as he can. Sure enough, I can see a smooth, round section of exposed scalp right in the centre of his head.

"What? *Jesus*?"

"Yes, *Jesus*."

"I've only really noticed it myself, recently," I say to Mark.

"I'm an atheist, Mom. And since when do you care?"

"I thought you said you were agnostic?"

"When was the last time we even went to church?" Mark asks, emptying his bottle.

"I just said that so you'd think there was a chance I'd come around," Sandra says.

"So you don't believe in God now, is that what you're telling me?"

As I turn to escape to the washroom, I hear Sylvia say, "What does Tim have to say about this?" but I pretend that I don't hear her.

In the bathroom, my phone rings. I answer it.

"I don't know who the hell you are –" I immediately recognize Angela's voice.

"Hello? Sorry?" I feel the sweat at my temples. Building along my hairline.

"Don't pull that bullshit on me. I don't know what you think you were trying to do –"

"I'm sorry you must have the wrong number." I want to hang up but I'm afraid she'll call back.

"It was dangerous. Sending me over there like that. Who knows what could've happened –"

I can't believe I didn't consider the fact that she had my

number. How could I not have thought about that?

"And it turned out the stupid apartment was already taken." She begins to cry.

"Angela," I say her name, but I'm not sure what else to say. I look in the mirror and stare at the top of my head. I move forward to take a closer look, adjust a few strands.

"Asshole." She hangs up. I look down at my phone and turn it off. I know that I've done something wrong; I'm just not exactly sure what.

"The turkey is delicious, Sylvia. Delicious." And it is. The dark meat melts in my mouth. "Honey, you *have* hit a homer this year." Mark's got a glass of white wine and another beer on the go. I've switched to the wine, but it seems too dry after the beer.

Sandra's mood has worsened. She's brooding. Sitting in silence, hunched over her plate.

"It's quiet without Jim and the kids here." Sylvia has placed a few roasted potatoes, some squash, a spoonful of stuffing and two dainty slivers of turkey on her plate. She's barely even touched it, but she must be on her fifth glass of wine.

"So I guess we can stop waiting for you guys, eh?" Mark says, his mouth half-full.

"Dad!" Sandra's fork clatters on her plate.

"Sorry, Sandy, it's just . . ."

"So they don't want children. Not everyone wants children. They kind of ruin your life."

"Sylvia, don't say that."

"Well I don't mean *ruin*. Maybe I should have said 'take over.'"

"We can still have kids. A kid, maybe," Sandra says, but it's barely a whisper.

"Aren't you a little too old?" Sylvia's got the bottle of wine next to her plate. She keeps filling her glass before it's empty.

"I'm not too old."

"*I* think we might be too old," I blurt out. We've never had this conversation. Once, a long time ago, on a beach in Costa Rica, we even made a pact to never have this conversation.

"Technically, we're not too old." She glares at me, and I don't know why.

"Think about how old you'll be when the kid goes to university. No one wants old parents," Sylvia says.

"That's true." Mark hasn't stopped ploughing down the food through the whole conversation. "I couldn't imagine having kids in school right now. It'd ruin retirement."

"You probably wouldn't even be retired," I point out. I'm not sure how Sandra and I ended up on different sides of this argument, but I stare at her and wait for her to look at me.

"I still feel young," Sandra says, but she doesn't look up from her plate.

I want to do something to confront her, but I feel like anything I do will backfire; that the gesture would either make her cry or make her glare at me again. So I jab a piece of turkey with my fork, slide it through the pile of cranberries on my plate and put it in my mouth.

Mark looks ominous standing over the fire. His face glows red, cut with shadows so specific I could trace the outline of his wrinkles. His eyes are like two glass marbles. He sways a bit. I wonder if he'll fall into it.

"Sandy says you guys aren't going south this year?" It was from Mark and Sylvia that we originally caught on to the all-inclusives.

I take a sip from my beer and shake my head, surprised that she brought it up with them.

"Look, if you guys need any help . . ." He moves away from the fire and plops down in the lawn chair next to mine.

"No, no. That's not it at all. Really." I wonder what she has told them. "We could go, if we *really* wanted to. It's just more responsible to take a year off." I take a drink and stare straight into the fire. "You know, with Sandra back in school and all."

"Sure, sure. Yeah. But –"

"Really, Mark. Thank you." We sit in silence by the fire. Sandra and her mother retired to the throw rugs in the living room with the remnants of the wine, and Mark decided that he and I should burn the last of the summer firewood in the firepit. Mark shifts in his seat. He groans, and winces uncomfortably.

"Goddamn. It's a terrible thing getting old."

"Is it?" I ask, because I'm not sure what he wants me to say.

"The body. The mind. Emotions even. It all starts to go." He takes a long drink of his beer. He's sitting to the right of me and his face is only a silhouette against the lake beyond. "It all becomes a war. Or worse, just boring."

"A war?"

"Every relationship you can possibly have with everything and anything. It all becomes a war."

He stares straight into the fire for a few moments. "Nothing lasts forever, that's the thing. There comes a time when everything becomes a job. I . . ." Then he turns to look at me and even in the darkness I can see the pain in his eyes. He wants to tell me something. Something huge: something that will change my life. But I also see that he doesn't want to burden me with this information, and he is weighing that. He looks back to the fire.

"But this," I say with what I hope is a lightness to my voice, "this is what life is all about, right?" All I can hear is the fire and, every once in a while, a light lapping of the water on the lakeshore. "There is just something about sitting next to fire and water like this."

Mark struggles to his feet and grabs a piece of wood. "It's just basic is what it is," he begins. "Hydrogen, oxygen, carbon dioxide and," he throws the wood onto the fire; sparks shoot high into the air, "and the deteriorating human body." He stands there tottering over the fire, and again I worry about him falling in, but now, with the way he's leaning – and that wild stare – it looks as if he might jump.

Suddenly, there is yelling coming from the cottage, and both Mark and I look toward it at the same time. Through the window, we see first Sandra and then Sylvia come into view. Although we can't hear them, it is obvious they are arguing. Abruptly, Sandra turns and storms off. Sylvia's hands slap her hips and she stands, frustrated.

Mark and I make our way toward the cottage. As we enter, Sylvia picks up her wine glass and plops down on the couch.

"What's going on?" Mark asks.

Sylvia doesn't turn to look at us. She hesitates. "Just girl stuff," she says.

"Where's Sandra?" I ask.

"I think she's in your car, Tim."

I begin to turn.

"But maybe Mark should go."

We look at one another. There is a determined look in Mark's eyes. I shrug and he hurries out.

"Why don't you come sit with me?" Sylvia pats the cushion beside her.

I stand there awkwardly for an instant but eventually go over and sit. The couch is too soft; I sink in and feel my feet rise off the ground. Sylvia is sitting on the edge of it, her elbows resting on her thighs, and she's staring straight ahead.

"Is everything okay? She's not going to drive, is she?"

Sylvia sits and stares. Finally she brings her glass to her lips and takes a sip. "You know, Tim," she begins, still not looking at me, "I like you. You're a nice guy. You seem like a nice guy."

"Um. Thanks."

She empties the glass. "I'm going to bed." She puts it down on the floor in front of her and stands. Without another word she walks unsteadily down the hall.

Eventually I also stand and make my way down the hall. Nothing has been cleaned up since dinner, but there is a certain stillness to the disorder.

When I get to the front of the cottage I peek out the window. Mark and Sandra are sitting in our car. Sandra's on the driver's side and they are both leaning far back and staring up at the roof and talking. Even from this distance I can tell that Sandra's been crying. I want to go out. I feel like I should, but then I would have to sit in the back seat and that would be awkward, so instead I walk into the guest bedroom and get undressed. My phone slips out of my pocket, and I pick it up off the ground and notice that I've missed two calls and that there are messages. I check, but neither is from Angela.

As I lie down, I clutch the phone against my chest. I close my eyes and see Angela, see her turning away from the apartment building and staring at me in the car. I wonder if she's figured out that was me she saw sitting there. I wonder if she's lying somewhere thinking about that, wondering who I am. I will her to call so that I can hear her voice again, even just one more time.

Under my hand – clenched so tightly to the warm plastic and glass of the phone – I can feel my heart pounding.

DINOSAURPORN.COM

pick up my glass and take a drink. When I tilt my head back, I have to squint for the sun in my eyes. The beer is cold – so cold – and I'm so hot that I can actually feel it cool me. I glance at those around us: the table of beautiful women in sundresses and sandals, a few couples, a table full of suits fresh from the office. It's early evening on a hot summer day. The patio is full.

"Just ask her." Mike won't stop looking straight at me. Even when he takes a drink he makes sure to look around the bottom of his glass.

"Yeah, but –"

"Dude. Ask her." He's got one of those disappointed smirks on his face. It's a particular twisting of the lips that

I know he's been working on since he was a kid. We've known each other that long.

"It'll ruin it if I ask her."

"You mean she'll say 'No' if you ask her." He sits back in his chair, arm comfortably slung over its back.

"I shouldn't have asked you about it," I say.

He laughs: one short burst of breath. "I don't really matter here, do I?"

"No," I say. "No, I guess you don't." I slouch forward, elbows on the table propping me up. I shouldn't have said anything. I shouldn't have ordered this second pint. I would've just kept my mouth shut if we'd stopped at one.

"She'll kill you, right. You know that?" Mike leans forward and touches my hand, pats it a little. It's a moment of affection that is rare, but he's still got that condescending smirk on his face. "Rachel will kill you if you get caught." He sits back, folds his arms across his chest.

I cringe when he uses my wife's name. It reminds me that she's real.

My favourite Internet porn site is called DinosaurPorn.com. And it isn't really a normal porn site; it's one of those amateur video-dump sites where users upload and share their own videos. The catch at DinosaurPorn.com is that the users are usually middle-aged and the videos are shot on old or cheap film and video recorders. Initially the site featured a lot of scenes shot on film, like Super 8 or 16mm, but it quickly expanded to include any grainy, non-professional equipment including surveillance videos and cellphones. There's also a specific section reserved for hidden camerawork shot on digital cameras where one (or both) of the participants is being filmed unaware.

Wednesday evenings are my DinosaurPorn nights. Rachel has her pottery circle and our son, Jordan, being eighteen, could be anywhere in the city on any given night except, of course, at home.

I walk into the office and turn on the computer. I pull the blinds and check the clock. Rachel has another hour at the pottery circle, but they never actually finish on time anyway.

I sit down in my chair, adjust for comfort, go online and open the site.

I spend a little time catching up on the new uploads I missed from the week before. I'm getting better at filtering now, at knowing which ones I'll like and I can even distinguish a certain style just by the thumbnail teaser. I don't mind grainy. I don't mind overweight, hairy. I like thinking that my porn could have been made by the couple next door. That conservative couple who you assume has bimonthly scheduled sex, when actually they're going at it in front of old, loud film cameras and cellphones propped on bedside tables. Mugging it for the imagined viewer. Shifting to give a better view.

My hands are down my pants, and I barely even noticed. There was a particularly good video uploaded on the weekend. A hidden-camera video that features a chubby girl with dyed red hair and her skinny, tattooed boyfriend. You can tell she doesn't know he's filming by how natural she acts. When the guy's going down on her she drifts away at one moment: her head turns and her eyes open and she seems to be remembering something, something to do at work, a shopping list. Anything. Then she closes her eyes and moans, gets right back into it.

I've always secretly thought that Rachel would approve of my watching this kind of porn. I've wanted to ask her if she'd watch it with me, but I don't know how. There was this night, five years ago, at a hotel in Paris when we discovered that there was a porn station, and we put it on as a "joke." Then we lay down on the bed to watch it. We started touching each other slowly, absently, as we watched. We kept it on all night.

The skinny tattooed guy pulls his head up from between her thighs. The redhead sighs and giggles as she adjusts. She gets on all fours and he gets behind her. He looks up to where the camera is hidden. It's brief, just a quick glance before he looks away. Maybe he smiled just a tiny little bit.

I surprise myself and come too quickly to grab tissues. I look down and there's a long, gooey line of it along my T-shirt.

I beat Rachel home on Friday, but only by a few minutes. I've got a few bottles of strong Quebec wheat beer and she's picking up some food-court Thai. She looks frazzled when she gets out of the car, clutching a grey, generic plastic shopping bag. Her short hair is dishevelled. It's only been a week, but I still don't like it. Cropped close to her head, barely any bangs. It's not that it makes her look older – it doesn't – it just makes it look like she's trying to look older.

I open the front door for her and she gives me a peck on the cheek as she rushes in. She heads straight down the hall.

"Oh God, babe," she says as she enters the kitchen. She tosses the grocery bag onto the counter. "What a shitty day." Her shirt is untucked, her skirt twisted in not quite the right direction. "People are mostly assholes," she says and lets out a big sigh. She leans back against the counter.

I can't tell if she wants me to go console her or to stay away. "What happened?" I ask. My wife is a sectional manager at a chain bookstore downtown. It often seems like her job consists of dealing with a continuous stream of assholes.

"Oh nothing, you know. Just general incompetence from the staff and stupidity from customers." She looks up at me and tries to fake a smile and makes this odd motion with her hand near her head. It takes me a moment to realize that she is flipping her absent hair. I can't tell if she notices what she's done or not but then she runs her hand through what hair she does have and ruffles it a bit. "Where's Jordan?" she asks.

I shrug. "Work?"

"Do you think he works, really?"

"He has money," I say. "He bought his own iPhonething. He makes the payments himself." He's been working at a pizza place down on Bloor Street since he was sixteen, but Rachel once found a joint in the pocket of a pair of his jeans and managed to convince herself that he was selling drugs. I asked her how many joints she'd smoked when she was sixteen, but she said that had been different.

"When was the last time you saw him?" she asks.

I have to think. "This morning," I tell her. He came down the stairs as I was walking out the door. I yelled "Good morning," but he ignored me. He already had his earphones in.

"Did you talk to him?"

I shrug again. He's eighteen, just graduated from high school. What do we possibly have to say to one another?

She doesn't say anything for a few minutes. She just leans back and juts her hip out a bit. She's filling out with age, but it's nice, like she's growing into herself. I notice that her legs are bare under her skirt. Her skin is pale, and looks soft, cool. I picture her legs as an image on a screen. Black and white would be best. They'd look milky. But the light would have to be right.

"Why don't you go get changed, have a shower, whatever. Let me get dinner ready, okay?" I say.

She nods. She's staring straight ahead at some point in the floor, her brow wrinkled. I walk forward and put my hand on her shoulder. She's still attractive. Maybe just for her age, I don't know. I can't tell if maybe that's just what I find attractive now.

She looks up at me and smiles. "Thanks, babe," she says and gives me a kiss, brushing my lips. Her lids look heavy, like she's just woken up from a long sleep.

When she's out of the room I pull the individual boxes of noodles and curry out of the shopping bags. I pull some plates out from the cupboards.

On Fridays, Rachel and I try to always do dinner together. When you've been together for twenty years, when you both work full time and have spent the past eighteen years raising a child and when both of you still cling to ever-slackening artistic ambitions (guitar playing for me, pottery for her), setting one evening aside where the only goal is to be together is extremely important. Sometimes we'll go out for dinner and a movie, sometimes we'll just stay home, drink a bottle of wine or some beer and eat crap Thai food from the mall. Sometimes we just fall asleep watching a movie. Most of the time, we have sex.

I open one of the bottles of beer and pour out two pints. I raise mine to my nose. It smells sweet and bitter.

"So I saw Susan last night." Mike leans one arm against the rail along the edge of the patio. His eyes follow two young women as they pass on the sidewalk. "This is definitely the best patio," he says, shaking his head. We've been trying to go to a different patio each time we go for a pint this summer.

"So?" I ask.

"So what?" he looks at me genuinely perplexed.

"Susan? You saw Susan last night?" I remind him.

Susan is Mike's ex. It's been just over a year since their divorce. There were dramatic fights, changed locks, broken windows, a suspicious fire. I spent many long nights at pubs trying to make sure Mike got home all right.

"Oh right, yeah." He takes a drink, licks his lips. Leans forward. "We fucked."

"What?"

"Yeah, on my couch too – we didn't even make it to the bedroom."

"Jesus Christ, Mike." I think of all those late night phone calls, all the melodrama.

"Well, it was bound to happen," he says. "As sexually compatible as we are." They had been on-again, off-again for years, but I thought the divorce was going to settle it once and for all.

"Isn't she seeing someone?"

Mike shrugs, snickers. "Some banker douche bag. I don't know."

"So what happens now?" I ask.

"Between me and Susan?" He looks at me like I'm crazy. "Nothing," he says.

"Right. Heard that before," I say.

"No, seriously," he says, and he does look serious. "I just wanted the last laugh, you know?" He shrugs. "All good things come to an end, my friend."

We sit in silence and drink. I'm beginning to sweat from the direct sunlight. Mike checks out women without even hiding it. I wonder if he's becoming an asshole as he gets older or if he's always been one.

"Hey," he says, suddenly remembering something. "Speaking of fucking, how'd it go with you? You go through with it?"

"What? That? Oh right. No. No, I didn't." I was hoping he'd never bring it up again. Last Friday Rachel never did come back down from her shower. When I went upstairs I saw that she'd fallen asleep in bed.

He laughs. "So did you chicken out? Or actually ask her?"

"I abandoned the plan," I say, but decide that this will be the week.

I leave the office early on Friday so that I can get home in time to set up. Fredfeelie, the username of one of the leading hidden-camera uploaders on DinosaurPorn.com – his wife has been covertly filmed at least a dozen times – wrote a blog post with tips on how to set up a hidden camera. I printed off the instructions last night but it's all pretty straightforward. My "safe place" is the laundry hamper. There's an outlet right behind it, so I don't have to worry about the battery.

I put the camera in and turn it on; I tilt it and cover it with some clothes. I walk over to the bed and check it out. Not bad. I figure we'll start downstairs. Maybe even in the kitchen. By the time we get up here she won't notice anything.

I lie on the bed. Position myself the way I think we'll end up and memorize it. Fredfeelie warns against not seeming like you're positioning your "subject." No arms on shoulders to make readjustments mid-act, et cetera.

"And don't ever," he warns many times, "look directly at the camera."

I walk back over and uncover the camera. I pick it up and play back the footage to check my positioning. It's not perfect, but it'll have to do. When I put the camera back down, I notice that my hand is shaking just a bit. I'm hard too, and pushing against the fly of my khakis. A little bit of sweat builds up at my hairline.

I check my watch. I have another twenty minutes or so before she gets home. I should go check my email to see if there is anything from her saying she's going to be late or not. I walk down the hall and play out the evening in my head, the way I hope things work out.

I walk into the office and someone is sitting at my computer. I jump a bit, my arms flinging out in front of me. It's Jordan.

He's sitting with his back to me and he's got his earphones in. I can hear the music faintly. He didn't even hear me walk in. I look over his shoulder to see what he's doing, but it's all just lists and numbers and meaningless symbols. Now he jumps, cringing in the chair.

"Holy fuck, Dad." He pulls at his earphones. Scowls.

"Language, Jordan," I've never heard him say "fuck" before. It's nice, in a way, because there was something immature about the way he said it. It was practiced, like he'd been waiting forever for the chance to swear at me.

"Whatever. What're you doing home?"

"I live here, I often come and go. What're you doing on my computer?" I'm angry at him, almost. I feel like he's using the spare pages of my journal or something.

"Nothing. Relax. Seriously." He's got his dirty blond hair long and shaggy, and he dresses in baggy jeans and T-shirts with skateboard brand names written on them. He owns a skateboard and he carries it with him sometimes, but I don't think he's really used it in about a year. "I'm synching my iPhone with my iTunes." He closes a window on the computer.

"You're doing what?" I know he's talking about his flat, shiny thing. His phone/not phone. "And why on my computer? What's wrong with your laptop?"

He unplugs his iThing from my computer. Shoves the cord and everything into one of his huge pockets. "My laptop doesn't have enough space for all my songs so I keep them on your computer," he says.

"That's not the point," I say. "And how much space is your iThingy taking up on *my* computer?"

"None, don't worry." He stands up, fumbles with his earphones and doesn't look me in the eye. He brushes past me. "And it's called an i*Phone*," he mumbles, leaving the room. "Yer such a dinosaur."

"What did you just say?" I ask.

He stops outside the door and looks back. He's blushing just a bit, but there's a grin there, hidden. "Ah, nothing," he says and turns quickly and rushes off.

I stand for a minute, staring out into the hallway at the space where my son was. That's the longest interaction I've had with him in weeks, months even, and I don't know what to do. It always ends up like this, where I'm taken off guard, don't know how to react, and he's short and abrupt and dismissive. It saddens me that I don't know when the last time I had a normal conversation with my son was.

I sit down at the computer. There's a Firefox window open and I see the sign-in page from Gmail. I delete my son's email address and am about to type in mine when I notice that the History is up as a sidebar. DinosaurPorn.com is clearly visible.

I hear Jordan's heavy, sluggish footsteps trudge down the front hall. The front door opens and then slams shut.

Rachel's about an hour or so late getting home. She didn't email, and I just have to sit and wait anxiously. Eventually, I hear the car pull up and go to open the front door for her.

"Sorry. I know I'm late." She's breathless when she gets to the top of the steps.

I lean over to kiss her as she passes, but she doesn't notice and walks right into the kitchen.

"So, I got sushi," she yells.

"That end-of-day-Duffy-Mall-discount shit?" I follow her into the kitchen.

"Yes, that *shit*. You know what it can be like there on Fridays. It was an hour wait at Thai Noodle, easy."

She goes to get changed and I uncork the bottle of red I bought, which I guess will go with the sushi. I know she's upstairs in our bedroom. I know she's changing her clothes, probably throwing them over the hamper. My heart beats harder and harder until I hear her come back down the stairs. She's dressed in her robe. Thin, silky, mauve. I bought it for her last year.

We don't speak while we eat our first few bites of sushi. It's all generic and more tasteless than raw fish and wasabi should possibly be. I'm missing our usual MSG-filled, North American–style Thai noodles and curries. I would've waited in line.

"This is disgusting," she says, taking a large drink of her wine. "But the wine's nice."

"So what're we going to do tonight?" I ask.

"What do you think?" She plops a long slimy piece of red faux-fish into her mouth. Some soya sauce slips over her lips.

I shrug; watch her lick the soya sauce. Wonder if I can just go over there and start kissing her now. Lead her up-stairs.

"Hasn't this just become our designated sex night?"

she looks me straight in my eyes as she says it and my heart jumps.

"Um, well, no," I say. "It's just a night for us to be together." I didn't think it had become that predictable.

"When else do we have sex?"

She's got a point. Our son hasn't spent a Friday night at home since he was fourteen. Or at least it feels that way, and we're always alone. I guess sometimes it feels obligatory.

I refill our glasses and we drink, both of us ignoring the last sushi roll. There is silence, and I wish I'd turned on some music before we started eating. Even having the television news on in another room would be better than this.

"So maybe I was expecting sex, but that doesn't mean we have to talk about it," I say and immediately regret it. "It just kind of, you know, ruins the mood if you talk about it."

She shakes her head. "What mood? Why the hell do you think I'm wearing this robe? Should I have dressed in layers to build the suspense?" She sits up, pulls her robe closed.

"Fine." I empty my glass.

After a few moments, she stands up and walks around the table. She shoves me a little and I push the chair out. She sits on my lap and the robe falls open over her legs.

She's not wearing anything underneath it. "Sorry, babe, didn't mean to ruin anything." She looks at me with mock concern on her face. Touches her forehead to mine. "How can I bring it back?" She kisses me.

I bring my hand up and touch her legs. Run it up along her thighs. She shifts, parts her legs. She feels damp, still, from the shower. Warm.

"See, it's back, right?" She leans back and closes her eyes. She pushes herself at me. "The mood?"

I'm shaking, sweating just a little. Light-headed from the wine. "Let's watch some porn," I whisper, and I don't even know where it comes from. It just comes out.

"What?" She closes her legs on my hand. Opens her eyes.

"Um. Porn." I think back to that night in the Paris hotel room.

"Why?"

"I don't know," I say. I can see that she's not ready for that. Not at the moment. "Never mind."

"What porn? Do you have porn?"

"No, no. Like Internet. On the Internet." Suddenly I look at her face and I can see her online. An image of her in grainy, black-and-white footage. The way her whole face elongates during sex: her eyebrows seeming to touch her hairline, jaw resting on her chest.

"No. God. Why?"

Now *I've* ruined the mood. I pull my hand away.

"You want me to watch your Internet porn?" She stands up, reaches across the table to grab her glass of wine.

"No, it's not that. I just a thought . . . Nothing." My wine glass is empty.

She stands there and drinks her wine, staring at me in a way I can't read. Blank. But not quite angry. I don't think. I don't know. She just looks tired.

And she stands there like that for a long time, staring not quite at me, but in my direction. She's taking sip after sip of her wine. Emptying it slowly. Eventually she turns, leaves me alone in the room. I hear her footsteps – her bare feet on the wood of the stairs – and then the creak of the floor above me. Faintly, I hear our bedroom door close.

THE KILL-IT-AND-FILL-IT GUY

he phone rang, waking me up. To get it, I had to sit up and reach over Sandy and fumble around the bedside table, around the alarm clock and the lamp and whatever book she was reading. I managed to grab the handset, but the receiver fell from the table and hung there, rocking against the table leg.

"John? It's me."

"Jesus, Everett. It's two in the morning. We gotta work tomorrow."

"Obviously it's important, I wouldn't call . . ."

"You been drinkin'?" Back when my brother was drinking heavy, he used to call in the middle of the night all drunk. "I'm not talkin' to you if you been drinking."

"I have *not* been drinking."

Sandy rolled over with a "hmph" and mumbled something in her sleep. My brother got quiet.

"I have bad news," he said and paused. "John, Dad's not doing so well." He paused again and I waited. There had to be more, Dad hadn't been doing so good for a long time.

"John?"

"I'm here! What the hell do you mean?"

"He had a heart attack," Everett said.

"How do you know?"

"What do you mean, 'how do I know?' Mom called me."

"Why ain't she calling me?"

"Christ, John, *ain't*? Don't be such a hick."

"It's two in the morning, Eve. I *ain't* thinkin' much about my words."

"Don't call me that," he said.

Sandy rolled over again with another snort. She whimpered a few times and seemed to go back to sleep. I told him I'd go downstairs and call him back. I hung up and lifted myself out of bed as gently as possible.

"Who's on the phone? Something wrong?" Sandy's voice was creamy like she was talking in her sleep.

I thought for a moment, then said, "Just Everett. Needs to talk." I didn't need her being all emotional. She didn't say anything else, so I walked out.

🦞

I sat down on the toilet and lit a smoke. I liked the bath-room. It was one of the only places I could really think. I rarely read, like others seem to. I decided to finish my whole smoke before I called Everett.

My family still lived in Nova Scotia. Parents in the same two-bedroom bungalow in Dartmouth I grew up in, brother living in his partner's condo across the harbour in Halifax. I knew Dad would be at the QEII right then. Lying in some bed, hooked up to a bunch of machines while my mom sat holding his hand. He treated her like shit, beat her and belittled her, but he was all she had.

Everett had more reason to be relieved than any of us.

When Everett was only fifteen he came home with an earring. He was already acting pretty fruity anyway, so it was no surprise to me. Dad freaked out, chased him around the house yelling that he was going to tear it out of his ear, my mom crying and begging him to stop. Dad ended up calling him a faggot – the first, but certainly not last, time he'd use that word – and told him to get rid of the earring or get out of the house. Everett got rid of the earring that night. Dad was a big man, an intimidating man. His forearms were the size of Everett's waist; his fist, Everett's head. Dad had always disciplined hard and often, but after that – even at his age – Everett got beat for anything and everything. That's also around the time my brother started his drinking.

When he came home after his first year of university in Quebec with a boyfriend, Dad didn't say anything to him. Instead he said some godawful things to my mom and told her that if those two didn't leave he was going to grab his rifle and shoot them. He said this with them standing right there. He wouldn't really have done anything so bad as that, but he said it and that was enough. My brother and his friend left.

It seemed that the worse he treated Everett, the better he treated me. I remember on my eighteenth birthday he sat me down after dinner and slipped me a Schooner like it was a big moment, like I'd never had a beer before. I thought Schooner tasted like shit, but I never told him that.

Then he said, "Listen up. Yer a man now. And this is the biggest piece of advice I can pass on to you." He took a big swig of beer and eyed me so I took one too. Then he leaned forward. "You ever notice that your mom ain't the brightest lady? Huh? If you find a smart woman, get rid a her. Never marry a smart woman, John. They'll be nothin' but trouble. They'll ruin ya."

I threw the cigarette between my legs, heard it fizzle in the toilet and stood up. I grabbed a can of air freshener from under the sink and sprayed it. Sandy hated it when I smoked in the bathroom, but we shit in there and I didn't see how smoking was any worse.

I grabbed my housecoat from the back of the door and put it on in front of the mirror. I was thirty-nine years old, Dad only sixty-one, and I'd inherited some traits. I liked to drink beer, smoke. And, as much as I hated to admit it, I looked like him. Same nose and body; well, not quite as big, but big enough. Same green eyes sunk back under my forehead, and a bum-chin too. I was even balding like he did, starting in the centre of my head, then spiralling, like the hair's getting sucked into my skull. I hadn't been to a doctor in God-only-knew-how-long, so maybe I only had another twenty years in me. I turned away from the mirror and headed downstairs.

In the kitchen there was a phone on the wall next to the fridge. The phone was old, but it had this gloss to it as if it'd been rubbed down before we went to bed. It made me notice the order and control of the kitchen, with everything in its place. I couldn't figure it out. Every day almost, I'd use something that as far as I could tell just sat wherever on the counter, and then Sandy would come around behind me and put it back in its certain place.

I took a deep breath, grabbed the phone and dialled Everett's number. It went five rings before a sleepy voice greeted me on the other end. It was Jason, Everett's part-ner. He told me that my mom had called and things were worse. My brother had left for the hospital right away and was going to call me when he got there. I apologized to Jason for waking him, thanked him for the news and hung up. Everett wouldn't have gone to the hospital unless things were really bad, like if there was no chance of Dad attacking him. They hadn't seen each other for a bunch of years, since Dad found out he'd moved in with another guy.

I put on a pot of coffee and waited for it to brew.

Everett was trying to be a poet, and things weren't going so good for him in that regard, but Jason was the editor of a gay monthly paper in Halifax – *Gay Times*, *The Queer Press*, something obvious like that – and Everett wrote articles for it to get by. Plus, he'd been sober for five years. So I guess he was doing all right.

The phone rang while I was pouring my second coffee. I wiped up some sugar I'd spilt on the counter while I answered it.

Everett didn't wait a second to tell me what was going on. "Dad's dead, John. Mom is freaking out. I can't talk right now." His voiced buzzed with energy.

"Wait, wait. Dad's dead?" I felt this little pang in my chest that I wasn't expecting.

"I have to go be with Mom. I'll call back when things calm down. Caroline is here too, so she'll help with things."

"Christ. It's over, eh? Wow." I didn't know what to

say. He hung up and I sat down at the kitchen table with my coffee. Felt like a big goddamn tire was just plopped down on my chest then yanked right off again.

Everett was upset: his voice was unstable, and I could tell he must have been crying. And Caroline was there, which would just make things worse. Caroline, my mom's little sister, was a total bitch. I knew right then she'd be on the phone calling everyone, taking charge, sucking in the sympathy like it was her who'd just lost her husband. And boy, did she ever hate Everett.

"God didn't make us like that," she once said to me about him. "It's unnatural and a sin."

"Whaddya mean 'God didn't make us like that'?" I said right back. "It works, right? It *fits*." I tried to laugh it off, but this disgusted her to no end, and she gave up on me after that.

I downed another cup of coffee and started thinking about going to sleep. But when I stood up I realized that I was loaded on caffeine and my mind was spinning with the idea that my old man was dead and everything that meant. Like a funeral. I wasn't sure I could afford to fly home for a funeral, not at the moment. And I wondered what would happen to Mom. Should me and Sandy offer for her to come live with us, or even just to visit for a vacation? I hadn't been home or seen my mother in over three years. When I moved away, I promised I'd visit once a year. I did for the first few years.

I wasn't doing anything spectacular back home at the time I left: working in my uncle's shop, drinking. I'd once dated a girl for almost a year, but then I got drunk one night at a party and fooled around on her. I was just going in circles. It was Everett who told me to leave, to go check things out, live a little, then come back and think about settling; he'd already gone to university in Quebec for four years and moved back home by then. When I moved to Toronto, I wasn't planning on staying for too long. But shit happens. I was there a year and a half when I met Sandy.

Things were just starting to even out for me and her, and we weren't fighting so much. We had steady jobs and we'd bought a house out in Scarborough, close enough to Toronto and big enough on its own that we got everything we needed and more. My work was starting to come together too. A mechanic by trade, I'd found it hard to get steady work. So when I first moved, I got into doing a lot of bodywork, repair, painting and stuff, and I turned out to be pretty good at it. I became the go-to kill-it-and-fill-it guy at the shop because I was good at working out dents. I had a particular knack for sheet metal lowering: taking out high spots created by dents, working them down, filling them and smoothing them out. Sometimes I missed working on the inside of cars, but there was just something about working on bodies. Everett says it's more artistic. I don't know about that, but there is something nice about being able to see your work when it's done. When a car drives out of the shop and there it is: freshly painted, that dent beat out of existence. Glistening. Engines can go long before bodies start to fall apart, and they got a mind of their own; all you can do is tinker around with them. Bodies though, they need us.

When I first moved to Toronto, I lived in Etobicoke, Rexdale actually, on the other side of the city. My buddy Derek and me had taken to this little pub near our place. We didn't have much else to do with our time and money and spent a lot of it there drinking beer and playing pool. It was a dingy little shithole, but comfortable and full of regulars like us.

When Sandy and her coworkers showed up one night, they stood out. I didn't even notice Sandy at first. She was regular looking: reddish-brown hair that she kept long, and she had these glittery green eyes. I don't know how to explain it, but you could tell by her eyes that she loved to talk. And her body was about average, maybe a little on the full side, but I liked that in a woman. Someone who wouldn't spend all her time worrying about how she looked in this pair of jeans, or whether she could wear this particular sweater or did it make her look too fat.

So I didn't really notice her until she and one of the other girls came over to me and Derek and asked to play a game of pool. I got partnered up with the other girl, Dawn.

"This is the leftovers of a staff party," she told me. "Us girls thought we'd go out for a little female bonding." We learned that they were all working at a security company's call centre in a nearby industrial park.

After Dawn made her first awful shot, we started joking that they needed a little manly advice. Derek got behind Sandy, who was playing right along, had one hand wrapped around her body, showing her how to square-up. The other rested on her lead arm to show her how to aim. She crammed a ball in the corner, across a helluva lot of green, and left the white perfect for her next shot.

"Gee, I guess I must be a natural," she said and went on to sink a whack of balls. That's when I really noticed her. You couldn't help but notice the way she moved around the table with that stick in her hand. She held a cue like it was nothing, just a part of her arm. And even to this day she is never more comfortable than when she's around a table.

I had no intention of taking Sandy or anyone home that night, but that's just the way it happened. We got to talking in the bar after everyone left, or she got to talking, I just listened mostly. Managed to get in a little about Nova Scotia, which she had never visited. I found out she played in pool leagues around Toronto, and won the odd tournament too. She told me about growing up in Northern Manitoba and her family and how she'd moved to Toronto to go to school and fell in love with it. She'd never left, nor had any intention of leaving.

When the bar closed, I asked her over for a drink. On the walk things got quiet.

"I don't usually do this," she said, hands in her pocket, shoulders drawn in. "Go home with guys I just met in the bar."

"Well I don't usually ask girls over who I just met in the bar." Which was the truth; I hadn't been with a woman since I'd left home. "I really do want you to come over for a drink. I didn't mean nothing by it." Which wasn't totally the truth; you couldn't help but think.

"All right, John," she said, as if coming to a conclusion. Then she laughed.

We hung out in the kitchen and had more than a few glasses of rye. The kitchen was a mess. We had this toaster that didn't have a crumb tray and neither Derek nor I ever thought of cleaning it. Mice used to eat the crumbs, but then we let one of the neighbourhood cats in and he caught a couple of them, so the crumbs started to build up again. There were grease marks all over the fridge, food lying on the counters and a pile of beer bottles and cases in the corner that had once been stacked but had fallen over and never been cleaned up. And the dishes, scattered among takeout containers, probably hadn't been done in a month.

But Sandy was drunk enough not to care and, before I even knew it, we were dancing around the kitchen. I felt like an idiot, there wasn't even any music or anything. But it felt good. She talked. Turned out she had just gotten over an engagement, her second. She admitted that she fell too quick and too hard for guys and ended up scaring them away. And in the end, I probably learned everything I ever needed to know about her that night.

"You got me drunk," she said, then kissed me, a little peck on the side of my mouth. We were dancing close together, one arm wrapped around each other, a drink in the other, and we didn't even try to keep proper time or anything. And then she started to undress, right there in the middle of the kitchen.

"Do you think we were supposed to meet tonight?" She pulled her shirt over her head first. I could see her nipples through her thin white bra. I wondered if I could undo the clasp or not. "I was supposed to be on a girls' night out," she said, pulling her belt through the loops. She undid her pants and stripped them right off. "You know, I even said to myself that I wasn't going to be with anyone. Not for a long time." She walked toward me still talking. "I really don't always do this," she said, but it seemed then – it was so comfortable – that we had always been doing this. So I reached my hand out and put it there on her chest and touched, just ran my ugly hands round in slow circles, as if I'd done it a hundred times before. I let her kiss me and start to take off my clothes, and if I wasn't so drunk, it would've ended right then. But it didn't, and we did it right on that dirty linoleum floor, her on top, little pebbles and pieces of crud scraping my back, me too drunk and fuck-dumb to say a goddamn word, to do anything but stare at this woman who I didn't really know, and think of cars, actually, and what a side panel feels like when it's had a dent killed and it's been properly sanded and prepped for a paint job.

Damn. I stood up, shaking my head to remind myself that I was on a clean kitchen floor in Scarborough. A new home, no crumbs on the counter, floors washed within the last week and grease marks wiped away before they got a chance to be stains. As I was walking around the kitchen I started wishing that we still did it like we did that first night. But things got real easy for us real quick. No more crazy sex on dirty floors or dancing without music. Fighting instead of fucking.

The phone rang, and I rushed to answer it.

"It's nights like tonight that make me want to drink again. I swear to God." Everett sounded pretty tired.

"Mom went to Caroline's. I tried to get her to come with me, but you know what it's like with Caroline."

"How's she?"

"She's not doing that well right now."

There was a silence then that I didn't like. "So, Eve, we got no daddy," I joked, because I didn't know what else to do.

"I don't know how to feel, John." He remained quiet, and I started to wonder if I was supposed to tell him, or if maybe I upset him with my joke. "I thought I would be pretty relieved," he finally said, "but it makes you think. You just can't help it. I don't know how I feel."

"Yeah," I said.

"What's it made you think about?"

"I don't know," I said. "Nothin' I guess. Lots a stuff."

"Like what?"

I didn't know what to say.

"I feel guilty about not getting to say goodbye," said Everett, "but I don't know why. I can't even think of the last time we had a decent conversation. Or even a normal one."

It struck me that I hadn't talked to the man in months myself. The last conversation we had was him answering the phone and saying, "Yer mother's right here." It seemed, suddenly, that this had all come on real fast. "I'm only twenty years younger than he is, you know," I said. "You don't think much about it when you're fifteen. How old your parents are. Shit, makes you think you don't have much time left." I heard him light a smoke and I wanted one too. "When's the funeral?" I asked.

"Are you going to come?"

"I don't know, when is it?"

"Think Sandy will come?"'

"I don't think we can afford it really, the two of us. She won't wanna go."

"What did she say?"

"Never told her yet." I pulled out a cigarette and lit it.

"*Haven't* told her. Why not?"

"Been sittin' here thinkin'."

"What about?"

"Nothin'," I said, and pulled my mouth away from the phone to take a long haul on the smoke. "I don't know." The two of us were pretty tired, I could tell. "What's Jason got to say?" I finally asked.

"Not much. He said, 'Sorry,' but he's probably afraid to say what he wants to. Like, 'At least you don't have to worry about that cruel bastard anymore.'" Everett laughed a weak laugh, probably because he knew it was true, and he knew that was what he actually wanted to say.

We sat there smoking, not talking for a while, like we were sitting together across the table, not halfway across the country.

"I think I might leave him," he said out of the blue, just like that.

"What?" I said. "What the hell for? You guys been fighting?" Another shock to add to it all.

"No, but I feel so dependent on him. He's my boss and I live in his place, and, well, it seems so final somehow. Like this is it, it's over. This is my life, and I haven't even lived it yet."

"You're too young to be thinking like that. Christ, Everett, you just turned thirty-three. It ain't the rest of your life."

He paused, taking his time like he does. "Well, I feel like I should have something stable, that I should be set now, ready. You know? Look at you, moved away, own a house, married. And look at me, thirty-minute bus ride from Mommy, living in my boss's apartment. And we feel like an old married couple. I already know everything there is to know about him." He paused again and took a drag; he was getting all excited, I could hear it in his voice, the way it rose just a bit. "I jerk off more than we have sex."

"Jesus Christ, Everett! I don't need to know that."

"Well, it's true. What about you and Sandy? You get all you need?"

"I guess . . ." I stopped myself before I gave the usual answer that everything was just fine. "I guess not. It ain't like it was, that's for sure. I'm getting old, though. Older. I'm more worried about that than how much I'm getting."

He didn't say anything right away. Sometimes, when calm, my brother thought real hard about everything he said. I appreciated that. Appreciated having a younger brother who could think things through for me.

"So what are you going to do about it?"

"About what? Gettin' old? Not much to do about it."

"Yes, there is." He said it right away, direct. Like there was something more to what he was saying, but I didn't know what. "You can do something about feeling old."

"You really gonna leave him?" I asked after I'd pulled out another smoke and lit it.

"Eventually. When I figure out how I can manage it." He didn't pull his mouth away from the phone when he took drags of his cigarette and I could hear it every time he exhaled right into the receiver.

We didn't talk much more after that. He was exhausted, and I was too, but I felt uneasy and couldn't sit still. I stood up and walked around the kitchen for a while, memorizing all the objects and where they belonged, starting to think no matter how hard I tried, I'd never figure it out.

I shivered, remembering that it was cold in the house. I rinsed my glass, put it in the sink then went upstairs to the bedroom. I took off my housecoat and slipped into bed, lying right down on my back, afraid to get too near Sandy and wake her up with my cold. Everything rushed through my head. I was so tired and yet so full-up with thoughts that I couldn't focus on anything and certainly couldn't sleep.

Sandy moved a bit, shuffled closer to me, and I slid over toward the edge. She smacked her lips.

"Wha's going on, baby?" Her voice was sleep-slurred, eyes still closed tight, lips bashed up against the pillow, and I got a little mad that she was sleeping so soundly while I was there wide awake, noticing the room getting lighter with every moment. "John?" she mumbled, but then was quiet again except for the steadiness of her breathing.

I didn't answer her. I didn't move. I just listened to her breathing and stared up at the light fixture, watching the glow from the rising sun slowly make its way across the ceiling.

SON OF SON OF FLYING PIG

*L*ast week a group of New Agers set up in Christie Pits and meditated in shifts next to the temporary garbage dump that had been set up there: frizzy hair and hoop earrings; stretchy clothes from Lululemon; beards and dreads and thick-rimmed, oversized glasses. They sat crossed-legged, lining the makeshift fencing around the mountain of trash. Facing inward, they closed their eyes and Zenned themselves right through the smell. I heard about it on the radio and read about it on a blog. The blog posted photos where you could see crowds watching the people meditating, scarves and hands clutched to their noses and mouths as they stared.

It's been seven weeks now since the city workers strike began, and the smell of rotting garbage is beginning to overwhelm. The odour hangs with the humidity. It clings to the hairs on my arms and to my sweat-damp T-shirts. It rises from the mounds of garbage lining the streets, stacked in absurd piles at the ends of driveways, overflowing from public bins on street corners and building up in the city's parks.

There are other important services down: no one's been married all summer, home renovations have come to a halt, permits for whatever needs permitting are not being given. In the beginning, that's the kind of stuff people talked about: daycare and summer camps. Now, just the garbage.

Our realtor told us that there was an elderly couple – the Hamiltons – living in the other side of the duplex, and on the day we moved in Mrs. Hamilton sat in her bay window and watched us intently. For the hours that it took us to get all of the stuff out of the truck and into our home, she never left her perch at the window. Only her eyes and the top of her head were visible, and her gaze followed our every move. At one point, I looked up and waved, and she waved back without hesitation.

Heather and I bought this place – our first home – in spring, and we were in by the first of May. We live at the end of a dead end just off of Weston Road in the west end of the city. Red brick, two floors, half-finished basement, back deck, a white picket fence down the middle of the yard cutting off our side from the neighbours'. The lawn is small, but the grass grows evenly and green. This summer I've taken to sitting out on the back deck with a six-pack and my laptop, streaming XFM, one of the local rock radio stations. Our yard backs onto the rail lines, and I know when all the GO trains pass. It's got so that I can feel them even before I can hear them.

I met Mr. Hamilton at the end of the first week after we moved in. It was warm for early May, and he was out back watering his lawn, standing with the hose in his hand and a smoke dangling from his mouth. He wore a pair of black canvas Converse sneakers, white socks pulled up over his calves, a bucket hat with a full brim, a pair of khaki shorts and an unbuttoned, multicoloured Hawaiian shirt. His skin was so white it almost looked blue.

"Mr. Hamilton," I said, trotting over to the fence.

He nodded briefly. His eyes were hidden behind a gaudy pair of sunglasses, and I couldn't tell if he was looking at me or the spray from his hose. I was wearing only cut-offs and felt very naked. I had a beer in my hand, and it struck me that it might've been too early to be seen drinking.

I stopped at the fence, shifted the beer to my left hand and stretched my right in greeting. He eventually put down his hose – the water still flowing – and walked over and accepted it.

"Jake Masters," I said. "My wife and I just moved in."

"Yup," he said, and stood there. He had a well-trimmed, white beard that was yellowed around his mouth where the cigarette smoke weaved through the hairs.

"Nice lawn," I said because I didn't know what else to say. The water kept rushing out of his hose. "How long have you and Mrs. Hamilton been here?" I'd still only seen Edna Hamilton sitting at their bay window.

"Twenty-five years." He took the cigarette out of his mouth and squeezed the tip of it so that the ashes fell flickering to the ground. He put the butt in his shirt pocket. "Lot changes in twenty-five years," he said.

I wished I could see his eyes beyond those sunglasses.

"Gonna be a hot summer," he said, turning. He bent down and grabbed the hose, his back to me, and resumed watering his lawn.

The strike ended up killing Mr. Hamilton before the summer ended. At least, that's what I joked. My wife said my joke was in bad taste. "Dead people don't have taste," I said, but she didn't laugh at that either.

I'd been laid-off by the time we moved into the house, and have drawn unemployment since. My old boss, Bernard

Gould, broke it to me right around the time Heather and I were finishing up the paperwork on the house. The business was Gould's Fasteners and Pulleys, and it did wholesale distribution and large-project rentals of fasteners and pulleys. It wasn't a great job, but it was a job, and I'd been there for almost five years working as a salesmen. He paid me as well as he could, added commission when I made big sales. His business was suffering before the strike: construction was down due to the recession. Sometimes I can't help but wonder if this summer has completely destroyed him.

I've been lazily looking for work, but there's not much buying going on, so not much demand for salesmen. The heat's been making it difficult to think too hard about work but easy to think about sitting on the back deck drinking beer, watching an endless loop of sports highlights and retro wrestling clips online, all with a soundtrack supplied by the classic rock on XFM.

The radio station is a major sponsor of the annual Toronto Summer Fest Parade, which is now being threatened by the city strike. I've been following the station's attempts to fundraise all summer to pay for the extra costs of security and cleaning that the city would have usually covered: the mayor sat in a dunk tank for a full day outside of the downtown studio, the Kids in the Hall did a reunion show that was broadcast over the radio and there is a concert scheduled featuring the Tragically Hip and other local bands.

This morning on the radio, they said that this was the longest we'd gone without rain in twenty-four years. Seventeen straight days with zero precipitation. I don't know how rain would affect the garbage, but it would give us some relief from the smell, that's for sure. It would knock it out of the sky at least.

Heather had a much more pleasant first encounter with Mr. Hamilton. "He wasn't nearly as bad as you said," she told me during dinner one night. "He was very polite to me." She plopped a big purple olive in her mouth. I could see her working to suck out the pit.

Heather eats gloriously. She's a decent-looking woman: thick and straight shoulder-length brown hair, and an indistinguishable face, except her lips. She has the most beautiful, full lips, shaped like a beautifully written capital *M*, that are a striking shade of pink. I watched her bring a piece of dripping penne to her lips, press it against them until they eventually gave way, her upper lip forming a sensual arc over the pasta, enveloping it. Her tongue worked its way over the tip of the pasta and drew it the rest of the way. Her lips closed on it, and they were damp with oil.

"He was even flirty," she said, swallowing.

"Old men like young women," I said. "They can't help

it." I looked down at the pasta on the end of my fork. I felt inadequate eating across from her.

"You're ageist." Heather works in the provincial tax office. She likes it because she never has to deal with the public. Just documents, she said, and they never complain. She was putting in long hours and beginning to look it. Her face was pale, almost gaunt, around those bright lips.

We ate in silence. I peeked up to watch her catch a sliver of red pepper on the end of her fork and bring it to her mouth. I shivered a little as it parted her lips.

When they were still there, Edna Hamilton rarely left her home. Twice a week a nurse came by to push her in her wheelchair down to the little parkette at the end of the street where they would sit and feed the pigeons that congregated there. Often, Edna would reach down for the birds as they ate. She would stretch out her hand to try to touch them, but they would always scatter before she could reach them, their little heads bobbing frantically, and Edna would sit back and laugh.

Aside from that, it seemed as if she spent the majority of her time sitting at the bay window at the front of her house. Because of the wheelchair, you just had this little rectangular vision of her from upper lip to her thinning hair. I actually felt bad that we didn't live on a busier street and made an effort to walk by and wave when I could. Once, after I waved, she brought her hand to her mouth and giggled. I could see it in the squint of her eyes, the shaking of her hair, and I couldn't help but imagine a once young and vibrant Edna, born into the world at the wrong time, fated to become an extension of the man who'd marry her, the children she'd bear. A life spent sitting at a window, watching while the world passed her by.

There are a million flies buzzing around the back of the Hamiltons'; the wasps don't even bother with our side of the yard anymore. There was a point around week four of the strike when I couldn't sit outside: the smell was too much. Now eight weeks in, I'm back outside and only catch a faint hint of it. I don't think my sense of smell will ever be the same again.

The contents of the Hamiltons' house are piled on their side of the back deck. It's mostly in bags, but there are nicotine-stained lampshades, half-rotting chairs and other pieces of old, broken furniture. Mr. Hamilton's shoes are lined up in a neat row in front of it all. They're mostly what you'd expect from an old man: faded loafers; a pair of grass-stained golf shoes; dusty, black dress shoes. But then there're those shoes he was wearing when I first saw him. The black Converse canvas shoes every kid standing outside of music venues downtown has jutting out from under their skinny jeans. I can't begin to imagine how Mr. Hamilton came to own a pair.

A huge shadow moves over the lawn. Like a low, ominous cloud has just formed above our house. I look up and slowly it comes into view from over the roof of the house: first the snout, then the whole head and, finally, the body. It's a massive flying pig. A huge, pink balloon like a float in a parade. On the side is written "Son of Son of Flying Pig." On the belly I can make out "97.7 XFM. X Marks The Spot." The pig is floating at a pretty good pace. There are long cords dangling from its feet. It's too far away to tell for sure, but I bet there are Steele's Heavy Wire Jaw Clamps at the ends of them. It's what I would have recommended when I worked at Gould's. I can't see how they would ever fail though, so I assume it must've been the fasteners. Faulty fasteners.

It was early July, just a few weeks into the strike, when we met the Hamiltons' son, Andrew. He stopped by one evening after dinner. He was tall and athletic in that I-was-a-big-time-high-school-superstar kind of way: he was soft and languid now. He wore pressed khakis, a greyish polo T-shirt. Clean shaven, his skin was near to perfect, with only a barely visible line of summer freckles crossing the bridge of his nose.

He explained to us that his father, who'd been suffering from emphysema, had caught another bout of pneumonia and was in the hospital on oxygen, and it didn't look good. He didn't respond much to our condolences and ended up walking away before we could think to invite him inside.

The old man lasted another two weeks or so.

When Andrew eventually took Edna away to a nursing home, I remember lying in bed, feeling inexplicably angry. "I think Mr. Hamilton wanted to go before his wife," I said. "He probably knew Edna wasn't going to last much longer and decided to get the jump on her."

Heather was undressing at the foot of the bed. She dropped her shirt on the floor and stared hard at me, wearing nothing but a bra and jeans. Her toes gripped the carpet. "What are you talking about?"

"He was selfish. He didn't want to be left alone." I shifted under the sheets, crossed my feet.

"You didn't even know them," she said, kicking the pant leg from her foot.

"He never once took her out that I ever saw." I crossed my arms. "He had that nurse come and push her up and down the street. He wouldn't even do that for her."

"They were married for, like, forty years or something. We knew them for a few months. Don't judge."

Heather got into bed and curled up in a fetal ball. I reached over and touched her bare shoulder. She didn't move.

Before I was laid off we had been trying to get pregnant. Heather had stopped taking the pill, and we were doing it whenever and wherever we could. We had to cool it after we lost my income, but she never went back on the pill, and we hadn't had sex for weeks.

"I'm sorry," I said, but I wasn't really sure what I was sorry about, or whether or not I even needed to be. I lay back and stared up at the ceiling. In the distance I could hear the 11:05 GO train approaching.

On the radio they've been tracking the flight of Son of Son of Flying Pig and have been encouraging people to phone in their sightings. The massive blimp – XFM's Toronto Summer Fest float – is caught up in air currents and has been making its way back and forth throughout the city. I glance up at the sky but see nothing but blue. Not even a cloud.

I look over at the Hamiltons' pile of garbage. Mr. Hamilton's shoes are still there. That pair of black Converse canvas sneakers, still in nearly perfect shape. I get up, jump the little picket fence and cover my mouth as I walk up the back steps toward the pile. Wasps and flies buzz all around me, but I grab the sneakers and rush back into my yard.

They are a little tight, but are canvas and, aside from the tightness, they are comfortable and certainly hipper than anything I've ever worn. I get up and walk around the lawn. Then I walk out toward the front of the house and begin to stroll down our street. I can't help but stare down at them and admire them the way you do with new shoes, feeling that silent sort of arrogance you get from new footwear. As I walk, I begin to imagine that I'm pushing Edna Hamilton down the street in her wheelchair. I imagine that I'm Mr. Hamilton, only he has his whole life to live over again, and he's decided to take his wife for walks, to love her with all of his heart, even if she is no longer the same woman he married.

I turn at the end of the block and head back. The shoes aren't stretching as well as I thought they would, and my toes are already starting to ache. I can feel a blister forming on my heel.

When I near our duplex, I am surprised to see someone in the Hamiltons' front window. More surprised that it's Edna. I stop right in the middle of the street and stare. She looks different from before. She's resting her chin in her hand; her sharp, bare elbow perched on the sill. She's staring off over my head, over the houses across the street, and I feel like I'm seeing Edna as she truly was. Reflective, sad even, slightly paler than usual. Today, she seems lost in thought. I wait and watch her stare into nothing. I'm moved by this, by seeing her capable of such simplicity.

Eventually, she looks down at me and smiles. I raise my hand to wave, and she looks straight into my eyes. She holds her soft, sad smile and waves back. Edna crosses her arms along the sill and rests her chin on them. As we stare at one another, her skin begins to shrink and soften; the lines around her eyes thin into the taut skin of her temples. Her cracked, deflated lips moisten and become full. The tangled mess of her hair begins to darken, then the wisps come together to form thick curls that bounce on her shoulders.

A car horn startles me and I turn quickly. One of my neighbours is waiting there in the middle of the street. He glares at me, raises his hands and shrugs. I move to let him pass. He pulls into his driveway and glances over toward my duplex and shakes his head. I look back up at the window, but it's completely empty.

Today on the radio, they say that the union has walked away from negotiations. The spokeswoman says there is no end in sight. She says that if the city isn't willing to budge, this thing could go until winter. We're about to hit week nine now, and the population is straining. There are daily protests at Queen's Park, people calling for the mayor's head. Rumours of legislation. Scabs. A man in the east end rented a backhoe and dug up his entire front yard. He filled it with all of his family's garbage and then covered it. If there wasn't a strike happening, solid waste management inspectors would have been called, and he might have been charged. As it stands, people are just thinking it sounds like a good idea.

After the news update, the DJ returns and gives an update on the Son of Son of Flying Pig. The pig has been spotted in my neighbourhood again. It's losing air, flying low and nearing one of the temporary dump sites a few streets over. In an ominous tone, the voice on the radio says that the pig's flight is becoming potentially dangerous. Authorities have decided that it's time for action.

The noon GO train roars by behind my house. I glance up as it passes, and then, out of the corner of my eye, I see it: Son of Son of Flying Pig.

Mr. Hamilton's shoes are the closest, so I grab them and pull them on, wincing as the too-tight fabric at the back rubs against the blister on my heel. I slip out from the backyard and head down the street at a brisk pace, following the pig. It has lost a considerable amount of air since I first saw it and looks emaciated now; the XFM logos on the side are crumbling in on themselves. As I walk, I see that others are also following, and still more are standing on their front steps, heads tilted skyward toward the Son of Son of Flying Pig as if this were the actual parade: a single, lonely float dancing wounded in the sky.

And then it's gone.

There's a bang that sounds like a gun, and the pig is tumbling rapidly, its body twisting in on itself until it's out of sight. The people who have been following it speed up and I follow. We round the corner just in time to see the blimp make its final descent. I'm surprised to discover that there are dozens of people watching as the massive deflated pig comes to rest on top of the pile of garbage in the middle of the park. There is an odd silence. Along with the spectators there are police cars, two news vans and still another from the radio station, XFM, yet for a moment no one moves or says anything.

Then, without warning, the deflated rubber carcass of Son of Son of Flying Pig bursts into flames and, within seconds, thick, black smoke fills the sky.

Heather notices the shoes sitting by the front door two days later on her way to work.

"Where did you get those," she asks and I tell her. "Why do you want to wear them? Christ, Jake, this is just weird."

"They don't really fit anyway," I say. I'm crusty with sleep, standing there in only my boxers. "They gave me blisters."

"It's just weird."

"Look." I lean against the wall and lift my left foot up, turning it. There's a torn blister on the back of my heel. Just a flap of dead skin.

She shakes her head and sighs a big frustrated sigh. "It just doesn't seem right to take a dead man's shoes."

"Well, what does he care, anyway?"

She puts her right hand on her hip and tilts her head. She looks sexy when she's mad because of the way she pouts those fantastic lips. "Maybe you should spend a little more time job searching," she says.

"What's that got to do with it?"

She clenches her fingers into fists then stretches them wide.

I smile, hoping to lighten the situation. "Heather, it's not that bad. I'm just going to throw them out anyway."

She shakes her head and closes her eyes. "Whatever," she says. "I've got to go." She turns, opens the door and steps out.

I rush to the bay window in our living room. She's already in the car. I stare down at her, hoping she'll look up at me, but then the car rolls to the end of the driveway and she pulls out into the street. I keep waving and stop only when the car is out of sight.

Yet even then I don't move. I stay and stare out at the houses across from ours, the trees lining the yards, the cars sitting in the driveways, the basketball hoops and the trimmed hedges. I stay there for a long time, beginning to see, with each passing moment, how interesting the world looks from here, framed as it is by the wooden sill around the bay window.

THE LADIES' ROOM AT THE VALLEYVIEW TRUCK STOP

They hadn't spoken in a little over an hour when she asked him if they were going to make it.

"I don't know," he said, gripping the steering wheel. The road had been the same for the last few hundred kilometres, roughly since they'd managed to find their way out of Edmonton. Northern Alberta had its own stark beauty about it, but, like the rest of the Prairies, it was a beauty that suffered from overexposure: stunning for the first hundred kilometres of open land and farms and yellow fields and cow pastures, but then monotonous after that.

"Is that a rain cloud up there?" she asked. Her elbow rested on the slim lip of the passenger window. Her finger, wedged into her mouth, probed the spaces between her teeth.

"Looks it." The clouds ahead had formed in a surreal way, as though rising from the landscape to meet the perpetually setting sun.

"Do you think we'll hit it?"

He shrugged. It felt as if they'd been chasing that sun for hours. Despite all the driving, it had not changed its position. And then a billowing white cloud had risen. Slowly at first, it looked like a mountain in flux, an anomalous geographical event. Darkened as it was by the dusk, it seemed only a silhouette, a massive amoeba-shaped silhouette, churning into itself on the vast Northern Alberta horizon. He liked the look of it, the excitement and danger it threatened.

"We don't seem to be getting any closer to it." Her finger fell from her mouth and she clasped her hands on her lap. Her posture was perfect: her back at a perfect ninety-degree angle to her legs.

They'd flown into Calgary on July thirtieth and rented an SUV at the airport. They'd then driven to Edmonton and spent the night there, stocking up on the required provisions before heading north. They were on a strict deadline, wanting to hit the 60th parallel before the first of August, their third wedding anniversary. She was convinced how romantic it would be, how the sun never fully set in the North at this point in the summer. "It would be like our anniversary never ended," she'd said. "Our whole trip could be one long day."

They'd left Edmonton early in the morning, the plan being to hit the Northwest Territories sometime in the late evening, allowing them to drive to a campsite along the Hay River and be settled by midnight. Then they got lost. One wrong turn led them deep into the city and their attempts to get out got them caught up in early morning work traffic, which slowly and painfully funnelled them out at the wrong end of the city. Once they got back through the city and on track, they were hours behind. She'd been on the verge of tears since that wrong turn. Pent up and ready to burst, he could see it in that absurd posture, the way she kept bringing her hand to her mouth.

He checked the speedometer. It hovered around 120 and they were making up some ground, but the gas was getting low. They hadn't seen a gas station in kilometres, since Whitecourt, and he wondered if he should have stopped there.

"What's the next town?" he asked.

She pulled the map from the glovebox. Navigation was her responsibility, though he wondered if he should have taken over that job after the Edmonton mishap. He could see her out of the corner of his eye studying the map with great precision, her finger tracing lines on the page.

"Where are we now?" she asked.

He looked around and saw farmland stretching as far as the eye could see. The odd patch of trees broke the flatness, but not enough to hide the depth of all that open space. Up ahead the cloud still toiled on the horizon, and the sun held its position in the sky, continuing to inch its way toward the ground.

"I don't know. On the goddamn highway."

"What is that supposed to mean?" she asked. "'*On the goddamn highway.*'"

He quietly took a deep breath. "I don't know where we are, sorry. You have the map."

"We passed Whitecourt, right?"

"Long ago, yes."

"Well, it doesn't look like there is anything until Valleyview." She settled the map on her knees and turned to look at him.

"And?"

"'And' what?"

"And what the hell does that mean?"

She remained quiet for a moment. He could feel her staring at him, and he knew she'd have that hurt look in her eyes. He would feel terrible if he saw it.

"I don't know how far we have to go," she finally said. The map lay upon her thighs. She turned her head to look out her window. "Maybe fifty, sixty kilometres."

He kept his eyes on the road. Stared at the cloud and watched in awe as it lit up in a silent flash of lightning.

The whole formation, for one brief instant, glowed yellow and became a huge fireball sitting on the road ahead of them. The lightning made it seem bigger and mobile and close. But he didn't hear any thunder so knew it was far away.

He watched as the needle in the gas gauge slid past the quarter tank mark. He looked up in time to see a set of headlights pass them by. A big truck.

"There were logs on that truck," she said.

"Yeah?" He hadn't noticed.

"That must mean something."

To him it meant that someone was trying to strip this bleak, desolate land of its one final refuge from flat monotony. There was nothing in his life that could have prepared him for this landscape. Born and raised on Vancouver Island, the only time he'd ever left BC was to go to university in Halifax. He'd been surrounded by mountains and the ocean for his whole life.

"Why do you think it's so different?" She didn't even turn her head, just kept staring out her window.

"What's different?"

"All this land. How is it so different from the ocean?"

It struck him that they'd been thinking the same thing. It unnerved him when they did that. He often wondered whether it meant they were compatible or had just spent too much time together. "I don't know," he finally said.

"It should really be the same, right?" She too had grown up on the coast, in Vancouver though, tucked away from the open ocean, hidden by Vancouver Island.

"Why should it be?"

"It's just open space. Flat, unchanging, open space." Her voice drifted as though just becoming aware of the landscape they were passing through.

Up ahead the cloud continued to explode every five minutes with an astonishing display of lightning.

"The ocean is less frightening," he said.

"How so?" She finally turned her head toward him.

He dropped his right arm from the wheel and shifted his body toward her. "With the ocean," he began, "you know what you are dealing with. If you walk right in and keep going, you'll drown."

She stared at him, and he could feel the space between them in the car.

"If you walk out in this," he flung his right hand out over the top of dash, "who knows what you're getting into. You could walk forever and slowly starve or die of exposure. If you're lost in the Prairies you can guarantee a painful, frightening, slow death. Drowning in a field of wheat."

"Land, land everywhere and not a place to go," she said.

This was the most they'd spoken in two days. Even when they'd had sex in an anonymous Edmonton hotel they'd barely spoken, moaned or grunted. It was irrational, but he hated having sex in a hotel. He always felt exposed, that everyone could hear him, perhaps even see him through some peephole in the wall. So it had been very businesslike. Missionary, quiet, without much activity. Simply a deed that needed doing.

"I think this is quite beautiful in its own way. I feel safer here than at the ocean. There's so much solid ground. It's so tame," she said.

"The ocean isn't?"

"Of course not."

"But this is all an illusion. It's all farmland and oil fields. Tamed by humans." He felt confident with what he was saying for the first time in days. "The ocean is free, alive."

"I guess so," she sighed, and he heard her head knock gently against the window.

They were coming up on a small patch of trees that lined the road about twenty feet back from the highway. He knew that this was also an illusion, the illusion of a forest, and could see the lights of a farmhouse tucked away amongst the trees.

"Hey!" Her head shot up and she pointed toward the patch of woods. "A deer."

He leaned forward to see for himself, and saw a small timid doe standing back by a tree, alert, head and ears up, staring back at them. It was too dark to see, but the animal's rigid posture made her look concerned. He could picture the look on her deer-face, worry lines creasing a furry forehead.

Then there was a flash of brown directly in front of them as a large buck leapt from the ditch. Her hand went to his thigh and grabbed tight, pinching his flesh there. His foot instinctively hit the brakes. They locked immediately and screeched, and he could see the buck – its antlers seeming to wave with all the motion – turn quickly. He pulled the wheel to the left, brought his foot off the brake and then the buck was alongside them, galloping, as though in a race with the car, confirming its manhood against the metal beast. It stared into the window, its head reared back, its big black eyes opened to such a point that they seemed as though they'd tear. Time slowed in those fleeting moments when the animal's eyes moved first to her, then over to him. Staring hard at them both before it turned and leapt back into the ditch toward its mate.

Her hand remained glued to his leg. His heart beat hard in his chest, and he could feel sweat dripping into his eyes. He checked his rear-view mirror to see the two animals bound into the trees. There was no traffic in either direction, so he pulled over onto the shoulder of the road. He let go of the wheel and sat back, taking a few quick breaths. She lifted her hand off his leg and let it fall into her lap. And when he opened his eyes he could see she'd begun to cry.

🌐

It was almost eleven o'clock and the sun finally hung just below the horizon. It had disappeared about a half an hour before, and since then had seemed to cease all motion. The sky was pink above it, a long thin line of light as though from a crack under a door. The storm cloud had barely shifted.

They'd come upon Valleyview without any warning. One streetlight appeared from behind a small rise in the road, and then to their left they could make out the lights of a small town. The road to their right blazed a straight path through a field and descended into the darkness.

He rolled through the intersection and pulled into the gas station. There was a K-car and an eighteen-wheeler outside a small diner. Through the window they could see a trucker sitting at a stool, hunched over a warm coffee. Standing in front of him, behind the bar, was a waitress decked out in a uniform.

"I'm going to go to the washroom," she said, opening the door and stepping out into the cool air. She hadn't spoken much since the incident with the deer.

He watched as she moved into the diner, looking so out of place in her long, loose skirt and sandals, her pale blue tank top barely covering the straps of her bra. She looked thinner out here amongst all this open land, pale and unhealthy. Her shoulder-length brown hair was tussled and uncharacteristically wavy. He watched through the windows as she approached what he guessed was a counter, obscured behind a wall. Then she reappeared and moved through small convenience store racks of potato chips and candy.

She kept her head down, her eyes glued to the dirty tile floor under her feet, stained with mud and fluids. She passed a coffee bar that reeked of old, burnt coffee and pushed through the door of the women's washroom.

The smell surprised her. It smelled like cheap room deodorizer: canned strawberries. She had been expecting worse. She went to the sink and stared at herself in the dirty mirror. A large beige flake of paint drooped down over the top of the mirror and hung there. She noticed that the paint all over the wall was peeling. She brushed some strands of hair out of her face. Her cheeks were rosy, and the skin around her eyes was red and slightly raw from being rubbed. She wished she hadn't cried. She'd been so pent up the whole time, it seemed, trying to keep things together in the face of his inaction. She had to make all the decisions. Had to keep things in line, organize everything, and still they hadn't made it. He barely seemed to notice, barely seemed to notice anything actually. And not for the first time, she wondered if her husband wasn't as intelligent as she'd once thought.

She ran some cold water and splashed it over her face, then went toward the stall. On the wall next to it she noticed a small vending machine that contained tampons and three different types of condoms. Gross, she thought. Who would ever need to get a condom from here? Then she remembered the truck outside and how long it had been since they'd seen civilization.

The toilet was stained a deep yellow, and in the stall, closed off from the rest of the washroom, the smell became worse. There was a massive hole in the wall behind the toilet and a pink blanket had been shoved into it. This damp blanket smelt strongly of mildew, and for some reason she imagined a baby wrapped in it. An abandoned baby born in this sad little truck stop washroom in Valleyview. Or born on the side of the highway, then wrapped in the blanket and deposited in the hole. But she dismissed the thought. Even though she'd never smelled it, she knew this was not what death smelled like.

She pulled toilet paper off the roll and rubbed the seat. She then tore off some more and lined it. But balling up her long skirt around her waist, she strained her legs to squat above the seat anyway. She closed her eyes and tried to tell herself that she was somewhere else, that they'd made it over the border and were camped along the river, huddled together in a blanket by a fire, sipping wine, sitting in silence and staring up at the purple sky, marvelling at the midnight sun. And they'd have sex, better sex than the shitty sex they'd had in Edmonton the night before, and finally – finally – she'd get a good night's sleep.

But when she opened her eyes again, she saw the grimy beige door of the stall and the illusion was broken. She was stuck in this truck stop bathroom, hovering centimetres above its plastic seat. Her eyes moved to some black writing scrawled on the door. In thick, childlike strokes, it declared that "Candace Wood sux dix." She snorted, surprising herself, then laughed fully. For the first time all day, she actually felt relaxed. Hovering there above a toilet seat, beginning to laugh uncontrollably while outside, seemingly a world away, she could picture her husband pumping gas from a rusty nozzle into the tank of their rented SUV, a type of vehicle he once declared he would never own.

He replaced the nozzle in the machine and walked into the station. One balding, unshaved man in his mid-forties sat on a stool behind the counter and looked up to grunt an acknowledgement as the bell above the door jingled. He stood slowly, pulling himself from the stool, adjusting his jeans around a heavy belly. It was undoubtedly a beer gut, as the man was, for the most part, quite gaunt. He had thin, sunken cheeks and bony arms that were all elbows. Even his chest seemed to sink back into itself. Underneath this, a solid round gut peeked out of the space between a thin white undershirt and the belt around his jeans.

There was country music playing in the diner, and the voices of the lone trucker and the waitress could be heard.

He gave the man exact change for the gas, and asked for the bathroom. With the shake of his head, the man behind the counter indicated to his right.

He slowly walked through the store and marvelled at the place, with its wood panelling and hunting apparel displayed so casually beside the usual corner store concessions. There was even a rack of cowboy hats against the far wall. He heard the water running in the women's washroom and wondered if he should knock on the door to see if she was all right, but decided against it. She was probably crying or something, wallowing; she'd been so shaken up by the stupid buck. It was alive for God's sake. They'd been in more danger than the dumb animal. He couldn't figure out why the damn thing had chosen that moment, the one moment in probably an hour that a vehicle had actually passed by, to cross the highway.

When he pushed open the bathroom door, the first thing he noticed was the vending machine next to the urinal. It had various condoms, but the last slot in the machine had a picture of a half-naked woman on it. She was lying in a bed, her bleach blond hair splayed out over a satin blanket. One hand was lost in the hair, the other rested on her stockinged thigh. The vending machine sold pocket porno-mags for two bucks. They looked like they could slip perfectly into the back pocket of a pair of jeans, or the chest pocket of an old plaid work shirt. He was shocked; he'd never seen anything like it before.

He walked up to the urinal. There was a bucket under it, placed there to catch the run-off of a leaking pipe. The stench of urine floated up to his nose, and he cringed. He kept his eyes on the vending machine. Two bucks.

She sighed and slouched in her seat, finally breaking her posture. She seemed much less tense after their stop. There was no traffic on the road ahead of them, nor behind. They hadn't seen any signs of life after the gas station, not even a deer hidden in the shadows, waiting for the chance to leap up onto the road in front of them. He felt utterly alone.

"I guess we're going to have to stop somewhere," she said, the first words spoken since the truck stop. "It's getting close to midnight."

"I figure we can get to Peace River." He thought he should apologise for not making it past the 60th parallel for their anniversary, but he didn't say anything. He was tired, exhausted actually. He'd planned on telling her about the pocket porn to lighten the situation. But he wasn't convinced she'd find it funny so kept it tucked away in his back pocket.

"Have you noticed the power lines?" she asked.

THE LADIES' ROOM AT THE VALLEYVIEW TRUCK STOP ❦ 241

He shook his head and looked up to see them. They were strange, not at all like the power lines he'd seen anywhere else. Instead of the cross-like shape he'd seen his whole life, there were three or four "arms" protruding from the top in jagged, almost triangle-like positions. They looked sloppy, as though they'd been thrown together by drunken power company workers as a joke: the asymmetry a tool to battle boredom and the repetitive nature of their work on this repetitive highway, in this repetitive land. But he quickly noticed that all of them were the same, exactly the same.

"Why do you think they're like that?" she asked.

He thought for a moment, wondering if they were more interesting to look at. And they were, but only for a few moments, and then the novelty wore off and they were like any other power line running along any other highway.

"I think it's for balance," she finally said. "All this open land, I bet the winds are fierce in the winter. Spreading the lines out like that probably helps keep them from moving too much."

He nodded and noticed they were headed into darkness. The sun had finally given up and only the faintest of light could be seen peeking out from the horizon. It reminded him that they were behind schedule. That, while close, they hadn't made it to the land of the midnight sun. Straight ahead, for as far as he could see, there wasn't one turn in the road or hill on the horizon, and even in the darkened light of this perpetual dusk he could see for miles. He wondered if the rest of the highway to the North was like this, if you could see it go on forever. It was unnerving somehow, the way it looked as though the road would never end.

ACKNOWLEDGEMENTS

A collection so long in the works has debts too numerous to properly repay, but hopefully these thanks will provide a start. First off, thanks to the Toronto Arts Council for financial support during the completion of this collection. Also, versions of many of these stories have appeared elsewhere, and I would like to thank the editors of *Monday Magazine, The Malahat Review, The Fiddlehead, Eleven Eleven: Journal of Literature and Art* and the *Dinosaur Porn* anthology. Your confidence and editorial insight are much appreciated.

I would like to thank Noelle Allen and everyone at Wolsak and Wynn. A very special thanks has to go to Paul Vermeersch, not only for the editorial guidance, but for trusting this work enough to allow it to help launch Buckrider Books, for which I am incredibly honoured.

I'd like to thank my peers and instructors in the writing departments of the University of Victoria and the University of Guelph. I feel ludicrously lucky to have had some wonderful teachers over the course of my life who have encouraged my writing habit and have had both indirect and direct influences on the writing and shaping of these stories. I would like to specifically thank Angela Griffin, Jill Fredericks, Heather Stephens, Jack Hodgins, Lorna Jackson, Bill Gaston, Michael Winter and Russell Smith.

I would like to thank my friends – from the literary community or otherwise – for the encouragement and for all the life experiences that inform my writing. I'm so grateful for having you all in my life, and I also feel so lucky to have too many to be named here. I would also like to thank my family and especially my mother, Judy Miller, for being so incredibly supportive of this path that I chose at such a young age. Your support and encouragement has meant the world to me and has guided me to this point. And finally, thank you, Jan Dawson, my partner in life and crime (IMTLY!). Thanks for absolutely everything, but most importantly for being so close beside me through it all.

D. D. MILLER is originally from Nova Scotia but has lived, worked and studied all across the country. His work has appeared in a number of journals and anthologies including *The Malahat Review, The Fiddlehead, Eleven Eleven: Journal of Literature and Art* and *Dinosaur Porn.* As the Derby Nerd, Miller is known around North America for his writing and commentary on roller derby, one of the world's fastest growing sports.

A graduate of Mount Allison University, the University of Victoria and the University of Guelph (where he completed his MFA), Miller currently lives in Toronto where he works as a college English instructor.

David Foster Wallace Ruined My Suicide and Other Stories is his first book.